POSH FROCKS & PEACOCKS

THIS NOVELLA FOLLOWS ON FROM COLD NIPS
& FROSTY BITS, WHICH FOLLOWED ON FROM
LIMP DICKS & SAGGY TITS!

TRACIE PODGER

Copyright © 2020 by Tracie Podger

All rights reserved.

No part of this book may be reproduced in any form or by any electronic or mechanical means, including information storage and retrieval systems, without written permission from the author, except for the use of brief quotations in a book review.

ACKNOWLEDGMENTS

Thank you to Francessca Wingfield from Francessca Wingfield PR & Design for yet another wonderful cover.

I'd also like to give a huge thank you to my editors, Lisa Hobman and Karen Hrdlicka, and proofreader, Joanne Thompson.

A big hug goes to the ladies in my team. These ladies give up their time to support and promote my books. Alison 'Awesome' Parkins, Karen Atkinson-Lingham, Ann Batty, Elaine Turner, Kerry-Ann Bell, Lou Dixon, and Louise White – otherwise known as the Twisted Angels.

My amazing PA, Alison Parkins keeps me on the straight and narrow, she's the boss! So amazing, I call her

Awesome Alison. You can contact her on Alison-ParkinsPA@gmail.com

To all the wonderful bloggers that have been involved in promoting my books and joining tours, thank you and I appreciate your support. There are too many to name individually – you know who you are.

1

"Well, what do you think?" I asked, twirling in my bedroom. My fluffy socks had allowed me to skate over the wooden floor, trailing my dress behind.

"Oh, Lizzie, it's gorgeous," Maggie said.

I was trying on my wedding dress for her. A month prior, I'd travelled to Glasgow with Joe just to have a look at some outfits. I had no intention of buying a wedding dress, let alone a vintage cream one, but I spotted the dress and I just couldn't get it out of my mind. Joe and I had visited various stores, some dedicated to wedding attire and some department stores. We'd pulled ball gowns and cocktail dresses from rails, in an array of colours. Of course, I loved them all but in the corner of a small boutique I caught the tulle and beaded arm of a vintage dress, probably dating from the nineteen-forties. I pulled it from the rail and held it up.

"Oh, Lizzie, that's amazing," Joe said, placing his hands over his mouth. The more he aged, the more dramatic he became about everything.

I heard a voice say, "That was my grandmother's." I turned to see the shop assistant, who I later found out was the owner, walking towards us.

"Wow, I'm sorry, I'll put it back," I said.

She shook her head. "It's for sale. She had three weddings, three wedding dresses," she said and then laughed.

"Was this the first or the last?" Joe asked. "I mean we don't want something unlucky," he added.

"That was the last and she married the love of her life in that one. In fact…" she laughed, "she married the same man three times."

I stared at her, frowning, even after receiving a slap from Joe to stop crinkling my forehead.

"She married him back during the war before he went off to fight. She thought he was lost in battle but he came home a year after, so she married him again. Sadly, they divorced; I guess the stress just got too much during those times. Many years later, and I mean, nearly twenty years, they met by chance, fell in love, and married again."

"What a wonderful story," I said.

"Is that true?" Joe asked at the same time as I spoke.

"It is, and yes, it's all documented. I have photographs of her in that dress. It wasn't new when she wore it; I believe it had belonged to an aunt or something. Anyway, she's still alive but she wants to sell it. She thinks it needs an outing and a proper wedding."

"Can I try it on?" I asked. The dress was super but the story made it much better.

It didn't fit, of course. It was a little tight and much too long. However, one of the great things about a vintage outfit was there's often spare material. It could be let out just a little so my boobs didn't look like they were about to burst out. As for the length, Daniela, as she'd introduced herself, could quite easily deal with that. She told me she'd qualified as a dressmaker at college and it had always been her dream to open a little boutique of vintage clothes.

"What do you think?" I asked Joe. He cocked his head to one side, walked back and forth and reminded me of Dave when we'd taken Verity's paintings to him. "What's that?" he said, picking up the train.

"A peacock, embroidered in," Daniela said.

Joe and I looked at each other. It was fate. "It was tradition to add something to the dress back then, a nod to the groom. I can do that for you as well, if you want," she added.

Joe and I spent the past week investigating peacocks. Initially, we wanted to just hire them but it didn't seem possible. Eventually, Joe came across a rescue centre. We hadn't told Ronan, who had forbade any more animals after the drama llama, the headbutting goat, Max with his wonky leg, Piggy, the pig with rickets, and two chickens that were more violent than all of them put together.

We had made a promise though. Well, we'd told the story of our wedding to Mrs. Sharpe and peacocks had featured, so I reasoned when I agreed to have a home visit with the prospect of taking a peacock and peahen.

As I smoothed down the tulle of the dress I sighed. "I'd like to buy this," I said, quietly. Even if it didn't end up being the dress I wore at the ceremony, I'd certainly wear it for the reception.

Daniela smiled. She asked me to take off the dress and then measured me for the alterations. We hadn't even discussed the price at that point. While I was being measured, I studied the garment. The detail was so intricate. I could make out birds and roses, all stitched in the same colour or created with beads. It was subtle yet when the eye attuned, what I was looking at was a wonderful garden. The sleeves were cream tulle, again, embroidered and with small silk covered buttons at the cuffs. The undergarment was silk and boned, fitted and straight. The second layer over the top was looser and fell into a train.

"Do you think you could add Ronan's name somewhere?" I asked.

"I can. That's quite a nice idea," she replied.

An hour later I was measured and then dressed. "We haven't discussed a price," I said.

Daniela picked up the label. "My grandmother would like three hundred pounds for it, but I'm happy to chat to her," she replied.

I stared at her, wondering if I'd misheard. That seemed awfully cheap for a vintage dress so detailed.

"We'll take it," Joe said, not batting his eyelids.

"Are you sure?" Daniela asked me.

"Absolutely, and I expect you'll let me know what the alternations will cost, nearer the time?"

"Of course, thank you. I think she'll be so pleased. Do you mind if, once it's all done, I take a photograph to send her? Grandpa died last year and I know she'd love to see this dress being used."

"I'd love for you to do that. We can also make sure to send her some official photographs as well," I said. It was on the tip of my tongue to invite them but apparently sensing that, Joe grabbed my arm and we left.

My small family only wedding had expanded just a little. Some of my old friends from Kent were coming up, which pleased me. My parents were flying over from Spain, and Joe was thrilled with that news.

"We have to put them on the same table as Petal and Eric," he'd gushed. He had been helping me with the seating plan.

A lunchtime wedding was going to take place on the terrace. The reception was then going to be held on the lawn. During the afternoon, there was going to be small tables and chairs, Carly, who had quit working at the hairdressers, was in charge, and afternoon tea would be served. A small orchestra would play some background music. Ronan had been in charge of the evening and booked a marquee and a local band, convincing me they were amazing for both pop style music and folk.

We had caterers coming in to lay out an evening buffet so Maggie didn't need to worry, but she had insisted on doing the afternoon tea.

"No one can make a scone like me and I'm blooming well not giving my recipe away," I recalled her saying with those short arms over her large boobs. When Maggie had her arms crossed that was the end of discussion.

Luckily for us, there was a very short break in filming the drama series at the castle so we could get married, and some of the 'set' had been left. There were four vintage vehicles on the drive; one of which was a Rolls Royce. It had been agreed I could have some photographs taken with them, although we weren't allowed to drive them, of course. When we'd signed the contract for the television series to be filmed at the castle, we'd made a point of stating there was one weekend that summer we wanted to be kept free. Since the pilot had been so successful, the television station had commissioned a whole series. It had been bedlam for weeks while they set up but the take down would be super quick, they assured me.

Maggie dragged me from my thoughts and back to the present. "Take it off otherwise it'll get ruined," she said.

I stood in front of the mirror. "I wonder what she thought when she wore this?"

"Who?" Maggie asked.

I told her the story of the grandmother and the three weddings; I thought I had already. Maggie's memory was a worry of late and something I had meant to talk to Ronan about.

"Oh, bless her, that's a lovely story. Now let me see this special message," she said turning me around and picking up the train.

Under the peacock that had a small amount of blue silk thread to highlight it, I'd had Ronan's and my initials and the date of the wedding added. I also had a small saltire. That was my *something blue*. The dress was the *something old*; *something new* was the sexy underwear. I just needed, *something borrowed,* and a sixpence for my shoe. Maggie was in charge of locating a sixpence. She had told me they had a little jar they'd put foreign or old coins in. Her foster children liked to use them when they played 'shop.' She was sure there were one or two in that jar. I'd originally hoped the peacocks could've been my *borrowed* items but that hope had fallen by the wayside.

"That's such a *London* thing," Maggie had said when I'd told her about my idea. "Hiring peacocks! I've never heard of such a thing."

I had laughed. "Well, you can in *London*, but, sadly, not here. Anyway, Joe has found a rescue centre that has some." I raised my eyebrows at her in a 'ah ha' way.

"It would be lovely to see them on the lawn. We'll be like those posh folks up the way," she said. I had no idea who she was referring to, of course.

My aim was to have the grounds open for one month a year to visitors. We had started to create a wild garden and were thrilled to learn we had a lovely, rare species of butterfly inhabiting it. Already, we'd had a team of photographers and experts pitch up and see if they could capture them on film. I'd done the garden simply to bring the bees back, but if a by-product of that was five pounds entry per person to sit and wait, in the hopes they might get a photograph, then it was all good with me.

I'd also been asked many times from location scouts if we had peacocks. I guessed, that *London lot* thought it gave the estate some form of credibility if we had some. I laughed when they suggested a dovecote and I told them the local falcons would make short work of those. It had dawned on me at that point, I'd lost that townie thing and had morphed into a country girl. I still had a lot to learn, of course, and was yet to shoot my first live animal, but I was getting there. I'd watched Maggie pluck a bird and my first attempt had resulted in lots of feathers removed, but also lots of skin and some meat. There wasn't much left to roast after that.

"Is Rich coming to the wedding?" Maggie asked.

"He hasn't been invited. I think it's best we don't go there. Same with Gregg," I said.

Ronan hadn't spoken to his brother since the day he called, pretending to be in trouble and off to America for the funeral of his father. Nasty letters had gone back and forth between solicitors until Ronan had relented and sent his brother some of their mother's artwork. He had been sure to pick out photographs and not the paintings. If Rich believed he was due half the value of the artwork, he could sell it and keep the money, Ronan had told us.

I hadn't agreed it was the way forward, neither had the lawyers, of course. Rich hadn't taken those images in full and final settlement either, and continued to try for more. In the end, it had taken a threat of harassment prosecution for him to back off. Although we hadn't heard from him for a month, everyone in London sure had.

Ronan, at that point, reminded Rich he had a stake in his bar and he wanted out. Rich was expected to come up with Ronan's initial stake, he wanted no more, and he was given a time limit to do so.

As for Gregg, it had been a foregone conclusion he wouldn't be invited. The man had slept with Ronan's first wife while he was still married to her. It made it awkward because Gregg was local but he didn't seem to care, which was a blessing. I'd also given Ronan my permission to punch him on the nose if he did turn up and disrupt things.

There was a knock on the door. "Am I allowed in yet?" Ronan asked.

"No!" Maggie and I shouted in unison. The dress was lying on the bed alongside my new underwear.

He mumbled something about being turfed out of his own room and needing the bathroom. We then heard him stomp down the hall to another one. Ronan was a creature of habit; he only liked to do number twos in our en suite, or the bathroom in the cottage. I thought that odd, I could poop anywhere without embarrassment.

"He needs potty training, that one does," Maggie said, and I laughed out loud.

"He's as much a drama llama around a toilet as that one out there."

Colleen, the llama, had been proving a hit with the campers we'd had so far. The kids loved the fact she jumped the fences, and would be wandering the campsite with Gerald trotting along behind, since she'd learned to let him out as well. She'd poke her head into tents and caravans demanding a snack and was getting as fat as a horse. She, and Gerald, were in their element, as if born for their roles and I often reminded Ronan it was such a great decision of mine to have them. We'd had a few reviews for the site and each one was positive and mentioned the pair. It appeared it was only Ronan, Maggie, and me the blooming things mucked around with.

Many a child had taken Colleen for a walk around the wooded area we'd designated for bike riding and strolls, and if they got lost, despite it being clearly signposted, she brought them back home.

2

"Oh, Lizzie. I think we have a problem," Angie said, when she called up from the campsite reception.

"Do you need me to come down?" I asked.

"I think that might be wise," she replied. I could detect a very slight wobble to her voice and wondered if she was upset or holding in a laugh.

"I'll be there in five," I said to her. "Something has happened at the campsite," I told Ronan. We had been sitting in the office catching up on paperwork.

"Okay, do you need my help?" he asked.

I shrugged. "I don't think so. I'll let you know."

I grabbed the keys for one of the quad bikes from the rack and headed out. We had invested in a new quad bike with a large basket on the back, and a tow bar. It had been a godsend using that to transport items back and forth. Maggie was banned from driving it, though. I was sure she was going to wreck the engine of the one she drove with all the revving and braking at the same time.

I pulled alongside the reception, a large wooden lodge that had a shop at one side with essential items of food, seasonal branded clothing and, the fastest selling items we had, fluffy toy llamas and goats.

"Hi, what's up?" I said as I walked into reception.

"Erm, caravan twenty-two. Their children strayed off the path in the woods and ended up meeting Petal. Not only Petal but…"

I took a quick look around before saying, "Oh gawd, don't tell me. Big Cock or Tree Lover?"

"Both, I believe. The parents are mortified and leaving. They're packing up as we speak. I think this could be a PR nightmare for us," she said. Her confused expression told me she was struggling with whether to laugh or be horrified.

I rolled my eyes. "Okay, I'll go and talk to them. It's not like it isn't signposted, it's in the brochure, and on a notice in all the caravans. I don't know what else we can do except build a ten feet high chain-link fence and barbed wire."

We hadn't experienced any issues up to that point, and since the naked art group had been meeting every weekend from the beginning of spring, I guessed we were lucky it hadn't happened before. The woodland walk route had been signposted well enough. One would have to stray some way off the path, climb through bushes and over a couple of fences. My phone was buzzing in my pocket and I noticed it was Petal. I took her call.

"I'm on my way to the family," I said before she could explain. "I'll come to you after."

"Okay. I'm so sorry, Lizzie, I really am," she stammered. Her voice was laced with emotion.

"It's not your fault, Petal. You're not to take any responsibility on this, okay?"

"Okay, I'll see you soon."

By the time I'd finished the call I was at the caravan. There were two kids that wouldn't have looked out of place in *Charlie and the Chocolate Factory*. In fact, I imagined one might be called Augustus. Both children's faces were covered in melted chocolate.

"Ah, there you are," said their mother. She stomped from the boot of the car to where I'd climbed from the quad. "My children are traumatised, look?" she said, waving her hands to her two smiling muddy and wet twins. "I'm sure they will need some form of therapy. I can't believe you advertise a high-class holiday park and have naked people running around. What would have happened if they'd strayed in here? Huh? Huh?" she demanded with her hands on her hips.

"I'd like to apologise, Mrs. Heggarty, Mr. Heggarty. We do have plenty of signposts to keep children on the correct path but we're going to review those immediately. We'd like, as a gesture of goodwill, to refund your stay. I see you're packing up, do you need any help with that?"

I had spoken as politely as possible without accepting blame.

"But what about those people?" she asked, pointing towards the woods as if there were about to be a charge of naked old folk into the campsite.

"They can read, Mrs. Heggarty. They have been part of the estate for many years. It's a sanctuary for them and they've never experienced children invading their space. I'm sure they're as upset as you are."

She opened and closed her mouth. "You'll hear more from my lawyers about this," she said, and her husband rolled his eyes. He gave me a wink and a smile when her back was turned. The twins just continued to eat their chocolate.

"Then I'll email you our company lawyer for you to pass on. Once again, Mrs. and Mr. Heggarty, we do offer our apologies that our signs weren't clear enough and we'll address that immediately. Is there anything else I can do for you?"

"No, we just want to pack up and leave, and I do expect that refund."

She turned her back and I took that to mean our conversation was over. Mr. and Mrs. Heggarty had been at the campsite five of the seven days they had booked but I would refund them. Not because I thought they deserved it but if we did all we could, we couldn't be accused of ignoring the *problem*.

I drove back to the lodge.

"Well?" Angie asked.

"I offered them a full refund, so I'll leave you to sort that. She's going to speak to her lawyer because she's convinced her kids will be traumatised." I raised my eyebrows and sighed.

Angie pursed her lips. "It was funny. When she came storming in, she was dragging one of the kids who was still laughing. Her husband was telling her to calm down and it really wasn't a big deal, the kids had seen worse. That seemed to annoy her more," she said, laughing.

"I guess it had to happen sometime," I replied. "I'm off to see Petal now."

I drove back through the woods and off to the art camp. Petal was standing with a towel around her waist; her pendulous saggy tits hung nearly to her waist and were exposed. I wondered if the tits were holding up the towel.

"Oh, Lizzie. I didn't know what to do," she said, and her eyes filled with tears. "I threw a towel over them," she added.

"Over…?"

"The kids. I threw towels over their heads. One ran, fell down the moat," she said.

I frowned at her. "The moat?"

I followed her gaze. The Tree Lover, bless her, had created not just a trench around her tree, but a proper moat filled with water, too wide to jump across. She had used old pallets to make a bridge she'd hauled up. She was nowhere to be seen, at first. Petal pointed.

Sitting on a branch was a naked Hailey. She waved tentatively and I walked over. I wasn't able to jump the moat and the bridge was up. I used my hand to shield my eyes from the sun and looked up.

"I'm sorry," she said, or at least I thought she'd said, and it was the first time I'd heard her speak.

"There's nothing for you to be sorry about, Hailey," I called up. "Are you okay? Can you get down safely?"

The last thing I wanted was her falling out of her tree. She patted the branch she was sitting on, and I wondered how her poor bum felt with the rough bark.

"All fine," she said. I nodded and left her with her branch.

"Is she okay?" I asked Petal, still confused as to why she needed to apologise.

"She's a little shocked I think. The kids startled her, they laughed and when they started to run off, they threw mudballs at her. That's why she scuttled up her tree."

"They threw what at her?"

"Mudballs, like snowballs?"

I understood what they were; I was just surprised the little *darlings* had done that. "Little shits, I wish I'd spoken to you first. Anyway, they're leaving now so you won't encounter them again," I said. I waved as I mounted the quad and left, absolutely thankful I hadn't bumped into Big Cock. "And, I'll be sure to mention that to their delightful mother."

I left then and headed back to the house. Ronan was still in the office when I returned and laughed as I told him what had happened.

"We'll put more notices along the fence. Not that we should have to, it's bloody well signposted anyway," he said. "And this lot called for you." He slid a note across the desk.

"Ah, peacocks," I said. He raised his eyebrows. "We told Mrs. Sharpe about our peacocks so we need to have them," I said, laughing.

The rescue centre wanted to bring forward their visit as they had someone in the area. I chuckled. No one was ever *in the area* where the estate was unless they were coming to visit.

Although Ronan had finally agreed to the peacocks, it had been reluctantly. "At this rate, we're going to need a bloody zoo keeper," he said.

"I need to check on Ronnie and Reggie. I'll be back with some lunch for you," I replied.

"Protective clothing, remember?"

I laughed and then headed to the house. Maggie wanted to collect eggs, we hadn't been in the coop for a couple of days and the chickens—we'd named Ronnie and

Reggie because they just didn't give a shit and ruled the roost—weren't *user friendly*.

"Are you ready?" she said, as I entered the kitchen. I burst into laughter.

When we'd transformed Christine, we'd found some overalls, a welder's mask, and a pair of welder's gloves. That get-up was now Maggie's egg collecting outfit. In addition, she had a lovely little basket over her arm that was lined with a beautiful yellow material and padded at the bottom to protect the eggs.

I pulled on Charlie's fisherman's waders and tucked the legs into wellies. I pulled on a short wax jacket, despite the summer heat. Protection was foremost in my mind, and if sweating buckets was a by-product of that, I wasn't complaining. I had a couple of pounds to lose. Ronan, of course, reminded me constantly of my *gimp suit* episode.

"Ready?" I said, Maggie nodded; already the plastic visor had steamed up because she hadn't prepped it.

We headed out. Even though he was in his office, we could hear Ronan laughing as we passed. Maggie stuck two fingers up at him.

We rounded the corner and behind one of the sheds, backing into the woodland was the chicken run. Before we'd got to the gate Ronnie and Reggie were at us, squawking and wings flapping frantically. They ran at us as we slid into the coop. I distracted them by allowing them to peck at my legs and feet, while Maggie grabbed the eggs. One—I could never tell them apart—flew at me. She could only get waist-high but her bloody beak was like a knife. If they could, they'd slash us to pieces. We didn't believe they were stressed we were taking the eggs; they behaved the same even at feed time.

"Fuck off, you little bugger," I said, quietly. They scared me and I wasn't going to provoke them further by shouting. I could hear Maggie chuckle. "How did we end up with these gangsters?" I asked aloud.

"They were free. Now we know why," Maggie answered in a muffled voice.

Answering me was her undoing. Ronnie, or it could have been Reggie, went for her. They pecked at her hands and she waved them off. That infuriated the bird further and the other joined in. I breathed a sigh of relief that I had a moment of respite. However, Maggie and I had practiced this. As soon as they switched their attack, I grabbed the basket and the last remaining eggs while Maggie drew them away from the gate.

We managed to get out fairly unscathed on that occasion. It hadn't always been that easy.

"I shall enjoy eating all these eggs," Maggie said, laughing and waving the basket at the pair who were still stomping up and down the fence.

It look longer to disrobe than it had to collect the eggs but, whatever it was with Ronnie and Reggie, their eggs were the best I'd ever tasted. I hadn't considered the taste of eggs before I ate real free range. They added a different flavour to the cakes Maggie made, as well.

Ronan walked into the kitchen with a shotgun over his shoulder. "Did you survive? I was giving you another few minutes and if you didn't return, I was going to rescue you both," he said.

"I can tell you now, Ronan, those chickens would wrestle that from you and you'd be running home with lead in your arse," Maggie said.

Tears rolled down my cheeks as I laughed so hard I started to cough.

Charlie arrived in the room. "Where yous off tae with that?" He nodded to the gun.

"I was going to save your wife, and mine, but they managed to survive the egg collection all by themselves," Ronan replied.

"Och, you just need tae wring their necks," Charlie said, shaking his head. "We could eat one while the other watches," he added, smacking his lips and laughing at the horror on Maggie face. "I'm messing with yous, we'll eat them both," he finished.

Maggie slapped him across the chest with a tea towel. "We have another wedding meeting tonight," she announced. That surprised me.

"How many meetings do we need tae go over the same thing?" Charlie asked.

"As many as it takes until the day. Now, away with you, I have things to do," Maggie scolded. Ronan and I headed to the office, and Charlie was in charge of the students that day.

"What meeting?" Ronan asked, as he placed his arm around my shoulders.

"I have no idea. As far as I'm concerned, everything's ready. She's excited, let's just go along with it," I replied.

Later that afternoon, we showed the rescue centre representatives around the estate. Of course, they could offer us the peacocks and were thrilled they'd be back on the lawn of a house they'd been missing from for over a hundred years. In addition, they started telling us about fundraising, or lack of, and the animals they had still needing a home. I told them I'd think about ways to help but right at that point, we couldn't house any more animals.

Ronan stared at me, open-mouthed and wide-eyed. "You bloody liar," he whispered still smiling as we waved them goodbye.

"Seriously, we have enough at the moment. But do I need to remind you how wonderful it's been having Colleen and Gerald?"

He walked off shaking his head.

Later that day we discovered the wrath of the Heggertys when Joe called in absolute stitches after seeing a review on our Facebook page.

"She said what?" I screeched as he read it out.

"She said you allowed perverts to run naked through the woods while also offering a camping facilities for families," he repeated, reading the review. "Anyway, my darling, I've put my PR hat on and replied. My reply has more likes than their comment so far." He seemed extremely proud of that.

It had taken me a while to find a suitable punishment for Joe after he had upset me by posting awful pictures of me on Facebook, and I was super glad I'd chosen that punishment. Joe was in charge of our social media. He had set up a wonderful page and we regularly filled it with photographs. We had some amazing reviews and then we had the one star we were laughing over.

"What did you say?" I asked.

"I explained we've had a naturists art group that has been part of the estate for many years. I mentioned Verity and some of her paintings that sold for tens of thousands of pounds, and I finished with the usual, no one else has ignored any of the signs or information readily given about the art group. No one has ever climbed two fences to enter the art camp and no one has then gone on to physically and verbally abuse some of the guests."

He huffed at the end of his sentence and I could imagine he would have been waving his arm as he spoke; he often spoke with his hands, and then slammed his palm on his thigh to make his point.

"They didn't exactly physically—"

"Yes they did! They threw mudballs. That's abuse. Anyway, it's her word—and when you read her post you'll see what I mean—against mine." I could hear the smile forming in his words and I laughed.

"Thank you. I don't know what the consequences of this will be."

As I'd been speaking, I'd brought Facebook up on my laptop and read Mrs. Heggarty's comment. There was a lot of support and a lot of likes and hearts on the post. But what I was over the moon to see, however, were the comments supporting us and saying *they* would be booking to visit.

"I can turn this into an amazing opportunity," Joe said.

"Then do it, please," I said, excitedly.

The filming and the art sales covered the running costs of the house. The campsite covered the cost of the students and the ground management. If we could add just a little more to either side of the business, we'd be in profit.

3

Whatever it was Mrs. Heggarty and Joe had started went stratospheric. Within a couple of days of their altercation on social media we had local and national press contacting us. Ronan told me that was when I truly came to the fore.

"I think we need a PR person to deal with this," I said, holding a stack of paper with requests for interviews.

Ronan gestured at the stack. "Look at what you've done here. You've set up a great website, taken all the photographs yourself, organised advertising. The only thing you left was social media. I think we have the best PR person we need sitting in this office."

"Me?"

"Yes, you! Lizzie, I have absolutely no doubt you can handle all that," he said.

I swelled with the joy his level of faith produced in me. "Okay, let me go through these and see what's needed."

Some were requests for interviews, where they'd send a series of questions by email and we'd also offer a couple of photographs. Others wanted to visit. Considering we had a wedding in a matter of days, I dealt with the email interviews first. They were simple. Most asked the same stock questions and got the same stock answers.

Petal and Eric were totally up for a small photoshoot and I was half-considering asking Big Cock since he was quite a handsome man, and it might squash the myth that naturists were just old wrinklies. When he demanded a fee, however, he was scrubbed off the list. I'd taken the photographs for the calendar the previous year, so I had an eye for it and thought I'd taken some wonderful shots where a branch with leaves covered certain parts of the anatomy, or we'd have a bum on show as someone faced an easel and painted.

I'd learned the basics of Photoshop, although not to the extent that Petal wanted.

"No, Petal, I can't make you look twenty years younger, or make your tits miraculously lift and stop looking like *dog's ears*. Also, I most certainly won't, even if I could, *pop a new willy* on your husband!"

Petal was sitting in the office with me scanning the images I'd taken. Ronan spat his coffee over his paperwork, and then spilled the rest as he knocked the mug to the floor while frantically trying to wipe his spit off the accounts.

"I'll leave you to this, then," she said, laughing as she left the office, thankfully wearing a robe. As she walked away, I heard a squeal. Gerald was in the yard and he'd headbutted her. She waved him off and her robe fell open. Gerald stopped mid-charge, in fact he skidded to a halt, and if a goat could show utter shock, he did. Those strange eyes dilated and then he keeled over and played dead.

I couldn't find a tissue to wipe my eyes that leaked from laughter so I dragged up my T-shirt and used the hem.

"Did you just see that?" I asked Ronan.

"No, I'm still recovering from what she said," he replied, not looking up from his soggy paperwork.

Once Petal had safely left the courtyard and Gerald had recovered, I returned to my desk.

"How did we end up with such strange animals?" I asked myself. I caught a look at Ronan from the side of my eye but I wouldn't face him. His mouth was open as if he were about to speak, and his eyebrows rose in shock at my words. I laughed.

Gerald, it appeared, was having an affair and I wasn't sure if Colleen knew. She was happily mowing the camping area, free roaming as we'd given up trying to keep her in a pen. In fact, the more she roamed freely, the less distance she actually travelled. She always returned for dinner and was so gentle with those she came across. The bloody goat, however, was the devil incarnate. That was until he came across Bess.

Bess was one of the working dogs Ronan had. She was an absolute ace at retrieval when he went shooting and so gentle she never damaged the birds she collected for him. Gerald was in love. He lay outside her kennel and sometimes we'd catch them touching noses. It was like *Lady and the Tramp* but with a goat.

"If he tries to shag our dog, he'll need to do more than play dead," Charlie said, as he walked into the office.

Ronan looked up, quizzically.

"Gerald has taken a fancy to Bess," I explained, quite casually.

Ronan shrugged but his expression was less than nonchalant. "Of course he does. I mean, it's perfectly natural, a goat fancied a llama and has now moved his affections to a dog, isn't it?" he said in a high-pitched voice that was overly dramatic in my opinion.

"She's gonnae have her wee pups soon, so we need tae keep the goat away," Charlie added. "I'm moving Piggy to the paddock with the bloody llama today as well." He then proceeded to grumble about the zoo we'd turned into, and that he was sure he'd catch swine flu when the winter came.

"Charlie, you love that pig. No one could get near him when he arrived," I reminded him.

Ronan had taken in some sows while their owner fixed their barn after a terrific storm the previous winter. One piglet had rickets and we kept him. Charlie named him Piggy, and I'd often catch him cooing at the animal over the stable door. Piggy had grown to a nice size despite his wonky legs, and he and Max had become good friends.

"We are the centre for the misfits, the oddballs, the ill, and the naked," I said waving my pen around. "In fact, that could be on our website." I laughed, knowing I wouldn't, of course.

"I'm just sayin' the goat needs his baws aff," Charlie added, then huffed and stomped from the office.

"Can a goat have his balls removed?" Ronan asked. I shrugged my shoulders. It wasn't like he would actually try to shag the dog, was it?

"Maybe ask the vet when he comes next."

With thoughts of Gerald's balls and interspecies relationships, we put our heads down and got on with work.

"The crew is here to dismantle the filming thingys," Maggie said, popping her head into the office with some lunch for us.

What she meant was the train tracks and overhead rails that allowed cameras to follow the actors, and the lighting rig, were being removed. We were expecting them the following day, but I was pleased because the marquee was also going up the next day and that had the potential to clash.

"Okay, do you need us there?" Ronan asked.

"No, just thought I'd let you know. I've made them all tea, they said they'll be gone in a couple of hours and be back on Tuesday," she replied.

I felt sorry for the crew but when they'd selected the filming dates, we'd made it clear we were holding our wedding on one of the Saturdays. An amicable agreement was found. They wouldn't have to move their kit from inside the house, they only used three rooms anyway, and they could leave everything erected elsewhere. It was only the front and the side terrace we wanted cleared.

"Oh, they left a wedding gift as well," she said, as she left us.

"I wonder what that is?" I said to Ronan.

"No idea, want to open it now?"

"No, we've told everyone no gifts so it would be nice to leave until the day."

Just a few minutes later, I took a call on the walkie-talkie from Angie.

"Hey, I don't know what's happening but we are being bombarded with calls and bookings. We're going to have to turn people away soon, unless you have another idea." She sounded out of breath.

I scrunched my brow. "Seriously? The interviews haven't been printed yet. Let me look at the Facebook page."

Within a few hours we'd had hundreds of comments and promises of bookings. It seemed some of those had come through with their promise.

"I'll come down," I said.

"I'll come with you," Ronan offered and shut down his laptop.

It took us less time to get to the campsite on the quad with Ronan driving than it did if I had been. He roared along, knowing every bump and pothole to avoid. I slapped his back to slow down as we approached. You never knew if Colleen or a child would pop out from the tree line at any point.

There were a few cars at the entrance into the campsite and Carly was managing them. She directed them to the car park where they then had to report to reception before learning of their pitch number

I smiled at her as we passed. She had proven to be a valued member of staff and she'd quit her other job to work for us full time. Although summer was the busiest, of course, we had activities and filming planned throughout the year. She was also planning a winter wonderland for the local children and any visitors who wanted to use the lodges over the Christmas period.

She was still a young woman but I had some plans for her, mainly business studies. Ronan and I thought she might be a great manager to take over from us should we decide to semi-retire.

"Hey, do you need help?" I asked, as I walked into reception.

Angie was running from the store end to reception to book people in. "Yeah, got a little busy all of a sudden," she said and then smiled.

"I'll take the shop," Ronan offered. He'd had training on the till and loved to play with it, regardless if there was a sale or not. Totally fucked up our stock and accounts, so Angie was constantly telling him.

I made my way behind reception where Angie was registering in a pre-booked client.

"Good afternoon, sorry for the wait. Have you pre-booked?" I asked a couple with three kids.

"No, we're doing a tour and saw your Facebook page. Thought this might be a wonderful place for a stopover if you have the room."

We went through their requirements. They were camping and wanted electricity plus one car parking space, a slightly larger pitch because of the tent size.

While the forms were being filled out, her husband spoke. "You know, it's amazing what you're doing here. I couldn't believe that old hag complaining," he said.

I wasn't immediately sure how to respond. I wanted to be professional, and I was also aware of how well the press could catch us out if they thought we willingly allowed children to walk around the naturist area.

"Well, I'm about to show you a map of the estate, something we do with every guest." I turned the map so they could see it the right way up. "Here is your pitch, and you take this route to get there." I drew a line.

"Where's the llama?" one child asked, bouncing on her toes.

"Ah, now, her name is Colleen and she's free range. Do you know what that means?" I asked, leaning over. The girl shook her head. "It means, she'll be sure to come and find you. But this area here," I pointed to the map, "is where you might find her. Don't run, though, because she might get scared."

I explained to the parents she wasn't dangerous, neither was the goat they might see mooching around. Ignore the pool noodles, we'd upgraded from pipe lagging, on his horns, he loved to butt adults but since he was tiny, he actually couldn't do any harm.

I also showed them a red ringed area. "This is our naturist park. You're welcome to visit but only if you're registered with their club and actively taking part in their activities. There's a phone number on the back. Their area has been part of the estate for many years, and we ask that you respect their privacy," I said with a smile. It was the standard statement we gave everyone.

"If running around in the nuddy is not your thing, there's archery, fully clothed art in the barn, swimming in the loch, although please keep inside the roped-off area, all the details are on the back," Carly stated as she walked past.

I laughed, as did the couple. Off they went and I dealt with the next client. An hour went past before we got a lull. Carly went to grab us some fresh lemonade and I was reminded we needed to consider some form of air conditioning in the reception lodge. We didn't have the heat waves to the extreme I remembered in Kent but it was bloody warm. I wafted air down the front of my T-shirt.

"Boob sweat," I whispered to Angie. She was a similar age, she'd understand. In the window I could see the reflection of my red T-shirt. There was a damp stain under each one. "I need to head back to the office, are you okay now?" I asked, as Ronan joined me.

"Yes, go, Carly can cover the shop."

Angie waved us off and we made our way back. I appreciated the speed that time, it cooled me down and I was sure not to cling on to Ronan so a breeze could waft down my T-shirt. Perhaps it was time for vest tops and sports bras instead of underwired ones.

"I might go and have a quick shower, I'm all sweaty," I said, as I climbed off the back of the quad.

"I might just come and join you, not that I'm all sweaty, yet," Ronan offered. "I also think we deserve a date night."

I smiled at him. "I'd like that." We had been working solidly for months and hadn't taken any time for ourselves

He wrapped his arm around my waist and pulled me to him. "I can't wait to officially call you my wife," he whispered into my neck.

I was about to reply when I felt something bump into my legs. I looked down.

"Gerald, sod off, will you," Ronan said before I could speak.

As if on cue, the goat did just that. He skulked off to the kennels and then got cross. Bess was out with Charlie. Gerald displayed his annoyance at being deserted by headbutting the bars. After that, he jumped up on a pile of straw bales and lay down.

"I think he needs another goat. Maybe he's horny," I said.

"I can tell you now, not that you'll take any notice. I'm not having a pack of fucking Geralds running around here. I also don't care if he's horny," he replied. "I do care that I am, though."

Perhaps Mrs. Heggarty had put a curse on us, but the following day, the glorious summer we had started to experience turned into the middle of winter.

"Jesus," I said, looking out the bedroom window at rain thrashing against the glass. "What the fuck happened to summer?" I said, despair laced my voice and it hitched.

"It'll be okay," Ronan said, as he walked up behind me.

"How are they going to get the marquee up today?" It wasn't windy but I had visions of having to sail to my reception. "Also, the ground is going to be too soft for the tables and chairs."

I didn't want to sound like I was whining, but I was watching my wedding to the man I knew I was going to spend the rest of my life with wash away.

He wrapped his arms around me. "We can move the afternoon tea to the terrace, there's enough room for the wedding and that. We can bring the marquee forward, closer to the terrace, and I'll lay a path so no one has to step on the mud," he said.

"You can't do all that work, and rest before the day," I said. Ronan had also planned to meet up with some locals, my dad, Charlie, and few others for a beer the night before.

My parents were flying in later that day and Joe and Danny were going to meet them at the airport and drive them over. I had wanted to but realised I was needed at home. That day, the set-up was to start and my mum had forbid me to be anywhere but at home. I was excited to see them.

"I'll do whatever makes you happy," he said.

I turned in his arms. "You do, regardless if there's a path to the marquee or not," I replied.

At that, we startled. Something hit the window, a stone. Ronan looked over my shoulder and laughed.

He pulled the curtain closed. "You just flashed those pretty, flowery knickers to Charlie and the marquee team," he said.

"Tell me you're kidding?" I begged, not wanting to look myself.

"Nope. Go and get dressed and stop stressing."

Plenty of women get married in the rain, I needed to take a breath and stop worrying. There were two more days before D-day. It was Scotland. Anything could happen. We could have sun and gnats, snow and ice, rain and wind, or any combination of them all, at any point throughout the year.

"We should have gone to Gretna Green," I said.

Ronan laughed. "Is the weather any better there?" he asked, then kissed the top of my head and smacked my arse.

By midday, the rain had stopped and the sun was out. I shook my fist at the weather gods and sent a silent prayer, if they could just stop mucking about for a couple of days I'd really appreciate it.

"Hello, darling. What a beautiful place. Now, where is that nearly son-in-law of mine?" my father asked, blowing an air kiss at me but diverting across the law where he'd spotted Ronan.

"Hello, to you also," I said, laughing. My dad was about the jolliest person I knew. He waved over his shoulder as he rolled up his sleeves to help Ronan.

My mother air-kissed me. "I have a cold and I don't want to give it you," she said, considerately. She then wrinkled her nose and sniffed. She lowered her head near my armpits and sniffed again.

"Mother! What are you doing?" I asked, backing up a step.

"I thought I smelt something strange," she replied.

I scowled at her. "Well it isn't me. Now, where's Joe?"

"Oh, he's faffing with the bags." She waved her hands over her shoulder as if she were referring to 'staff.'

I laughed when I saw the pile of bags and suitcases at the boot of his car.

"You make yourself at home, Mum. I'll go and help Joe with all your bags," I said with raised eyebrows and a very obvious sarcastic tone to my voice.

"Oh, thank you. I'll go and find Maggie."

Off she went calling out for Mags as she did. They'd spoken over FaceTime before and I'd had to pretend we'd lost signal to get them to shut up! Ronan and I hadn't had the chance to speak to either of my parents, as the whole time the two women had chatted like they were lifelong friends who hadn't seen each other for a while.

"Jesus, Lizzie. How long is she staying for?" Joe grumbled while Danny held out his hands for a hug. I was a little taken aback as he wasn't a tactile person normally.

"Hopefully, just a couple of days."

Joe took two suitcases, one in each hand, and I grabbed another and an overnight bag. I slung her handbag over my shoulder and waddled into the house. I left the luggage at the bottom of the stairs, though.

Joe and Danny took their *one* case and a suit carrier up to the bedroom they'd decided was theirs. I'd put my mum and dad in a room farther down the hall. Ronan had suggested we use his mother's room but we hadn't the time to box up her remaining personal items. It was one of those jobs we hadn't rushed into, although it had been a couple of years since her death. Maggie and I would go into the room to clean but it didn't feel right to remove the remains of her perfume from the dressing table, or the antique silver brush and mirror that had been passed down through generations of her family. We'd have to do it, at some point, but it wasn't high on the list.

Also, I'd prefer them not to be next door to me. My parents were rather vocal when alone in their bedroom!

It was half an hour later that I caught up with Mum in the kitchen. She was sipping on a cup of tea and she and Maggie were chatting like old pals. Joe and Danny were looking on, bemused.

"Is there anything you want me to do?" she asked with a beaming smile.

"You can come and look at my dress if you like?" I replied.

We all made our way upstairs. Joe had seen it, obviously, but he and Danny wanted to join in.

Mum placed her hands over her mouth when she saw it hanging over the back of a spare bedroom door. "It's beautiful," she whispered. I showed her the back and the personalisation I'd had done.

I was distracted, though, when Ronan shouted up that we had visitors. I frowned and stared at Maggie as if she might know. She shrugged her shoulders, as clueless as I was. We left the dress and headed for the front to see a small white van.

"Oh, it's the peacocks!" I said. I had forgotten which day they were coming to us.

The charity had made a temporary pen for them so they could acclimatise to their new environment. I thought they'd simply drop them off, and if we fed them regularly, they'd stay. Apparently it wasn't quite like that. I chuckled at the memory as I walked over.

"Hi, this is exciting," I said. The peacock and peahen were in the pen and I was thrilled to see him displaying already. Ronan and my dad stood to one side.

"This house just needs some peacocks," my mother said with some authority, although she was someone who had only ever lived in suburbia or an apartment in Spain.

We signed some paperwork, handed over a donation and then the birds were ours. Max had followed us and sat staring at them, he wasn't sure what to make of the peacock, particularly when he spread his feathers. Max backed off a little and I was pleased to see that. I didn't want him to harass the birds when they were allowed to roam. How they'd fare against Gerald or Colleen was another matter, of course.

"We'll leave them in the pen for a week then let them out during the daytime for a while, see how they get on," Ronan said, before he and Dad headed back to the marquee.

Later that evening while we were all sitting around the dining table, using the family crockery, my parents had us all in stitches. I'd forgotten how funny they were and shocked by how unembarrassed I was. I guessed, having spent time on the estate with Petal and Eric, I just didn't care anymore, and they weren't a patch on Verity, of course.

Mum and I stood side by side and washed the crockery by hand, she had sent Maggie off with coffee into the living room, and it had been amusing to watch a battle for territory develop over the kitchen.

"I can't tell you, baby girl, how pleased your dad and I for you," Mum said, using a term she hadn't in years.

I bumped shoulders with her. "Thanks, Mum. I can't wait for this wedding. I don't think I felt this way with Harry. Ronan seems to…it's too clichéd to say he completes me but he does."

She chuckled. "I know what you mean. Your dad might be a silly old fart most times but I can't imagine life without him. I hope you get many years together," she said, and then smiled.

We headed to the living room and joined the rest with coffee and more chat about respective lives and nudity.

As I had done many times, I sat back into the corner of the sofa and just observed. I watched laughter and happiness. I felt the warm glow of friends and family that got on so well and I let it wash over me.

"Are you crying?" Ronan whispered.

I hadn't realised I was until he'd mentioned it. I felt wet tracks on my cheeks and wiped them away. "I'm happy. Just…super happy," I said, and then laughed.

"She was always a crier, was my Elizabeth. Didn't matter if she was happy or sad, watching a scary or sad movie, she always shed tears," my dad said. I hadn't noticed everyone was watching me.

"I'm happy, these are happy tears, and I'm hormonal and menopausal and…so bloody in love with this man!" I gave my explanation.

"I think that's our cue to leave the lovebirds to make out," Mum said. Charlie spat out his tea.

"Mother! We are not about to *make out* so you're fine to finish your coffee."

4

It was the day before the wedding. The campsite was full and we were, regrettably, turning people away. I wanted to curse the Heggartys and cuddle them at the same time. The news stations had been reporting on our *Staycation for all, the clothed or unclothed,* and on the whole the response had been overwhelmingly flattering. Of course, Mrs. Heggarty had managed to snatch a few minutes of airtime and it was with great pleasure we saw the reporter ask the twins what happened. One just shrugged and the other explained they threw mudballs at the weirdos. That earned a slap from their mother and more kudos for us.

"You need to take a break," Mum said, coming into the office.

"I have so much to do, Mum. I will, later," I replied, taking the camomile tea she'd brought in with her.

Although the office was empty, save for the two of us, she looked around and whispered, dramatically, "I thought that might help, you know…with your problem."

"My menopause?" I asked, not sure camomile tea would do anything for that.

"You're a little smelly…down below…darling," she explained.

I sat, mouth open and wide-eyed glaring at her. I don't think my mother had ever offered any personal advice before and I also wasn't sure it was welcomed.

"Anyway, I'll leave you to your work. The boys are out tonight, aren't they? We have a lovely pamper evening in store for you," she said, giving me a wink before leaving.

"What the…?" I hadn't finished my sentence before I stood and rushed from the room.

I headed to the outside loo not caring about spiders or mice or any other critters. I pulled the door closed and immediately undid my jeans. I used my hand to waft but couldn't smell anything. No one had mentioned a smell about me before. I was sure that Mags would, or Ronan, or Joe even. My cheeks were flaming at that point. I refastened my jeans and headed for the house. I bounded up the stairs and slid around the corner coming to rest in Ronan's chest.

"Where's the fire?" He laughed.

"I smell, don't I?" I blurted out.

"Huh?"

"My mum just informed me I have an odour, from down below," I said, pointing to my crotch.

"Why is your mum sniffing…?"

"She isn't, she just announced it when she brought me a tea. Why didn't you say anything?" I asked, as we headed to the bedroom.

"Because you don't."

"Are you sure?"

I closed the bedroom door and whipped off my jeans; I wasn't about to sniff my hooha, but I did instruct Ronan to search the Internet and see if a sniffy hooha was part of the menopause. He couldn't help but chuckle as he did, complaining if he ever lost his phone, he pitied the person who checked his history. I headed to the bathroom for a pits and bits wash.

"Lizzie, there's an article to say that all vaginas should have a slight odour and that you're not to worry. You're also not to use soap or any of that shit because that can make your partner ill," he shouted through the door.

I opened it. "It says I can make you ill?" I reached out to grab his phone.

His lips were curled into that wonky smile I loved so much. "Okay, so it doesn't say that you'll make me ill, but no man wants a mouthful of shower gel. Now, I have no idea what your mum is on about, maybe she's been sniffing something she shouldn't, but you don't smell, okay?"

"Are you sure?" I asked, again.

"Positive. I can be more certain if you let me have a look." His eyebrows rose in question.

Since I was standing naked anyway, I thought it perfectly sensible to oblige. I started to laugh as I sat on the edge of the bed and he kneeled in front of me.

Before he got to work *examining* me, as he called it. He kissed my stomach. "Nope, no smell other than you and me and love."

———

As the day wore on, I became more excited. There wasn't anything left for me to do on the estate; it was manned by the students, one of whom was covering for Angie the following day. I took a walk around the side of the house to the terrace. It overlooked part of the lawn, the peacocks, and into the woodland beyond. At one end was a metal arch that would be decorated with flowers early the following morning. White metal bistro tables and chairs were set out, we had decided to forgo the usual rows and just have a casual set-up ready for the afternoon tea that would follow.

Ronan, as promised, had rigged up a wooden planked walkway from the terrace to the marquee. I walked along it, stood alone in the space and slowly circled. At one end was a stage and dance floor, at the other were more tables and chairs and a bar. I was looking forward to the local band Ronan had booked.

I'd taken a call from the vicar to check on some final details, and then I settled down in the kitchen for five minutes of peace. I think I got about three.

"Lizzie!" I heard my mum call. "I'm being held hostage."

I raised my eyebrows and took another sip of tea. "Lizzie?" my mother shouted again.

I smiled, placed my tea on the table, and then walked to the back door. "Gerald, get away from Nanny," I said.

Gerald was down on his front knees, revving his hind legs in preparation to attack.

"He won't let me pass," she said.

"Then just let him headbutt you, it doesn't hurt," I replied.

My mother waved her arms at him, *shooing* at the same time. That did nothing but to anger Gerald more. "Only you could have a mean goat," she grumbled and I laughed.

I walked over and grabbed Gerald by the horns. He was surprised to have his *attack* interrupted and proceeded to bleat to tell me so.

"Why aren't you in the paddock?" I mumbled to him, not that I expected an answer, of course.

Luckily, Colleen came calling.

"What on earth is that?" Mum asked, standing on the step to the back door.

"A llama. And don't be mean, she'll hear you. We also have two violent chickens and a pig with rickets." I let go of Gerald and he sidled up to Colleen. She nuzzled him and with a *harrumph,* off they trotted.

"Do they just run around?" Mum asked, horrified.

"Yes, they're free range." I chuckled as I made my way back to the kitchen.

"You won't want them around tomorrow," she added.

I hadn't thought about them and the wedding. They rarely ventured around the house to the front and I didn't feel they'd do any wrong.

I hoped.

In all the chaos that had occurred that day, I realised, I hadn't spent any time with Ronan. It wasn't until we'd taken ourselves to bed that we managed to get some 'alone time.'

"How are you feeling?" I asked, as he prepared for bed.

"Exhausted. I don't think I'll do this again in a hurry." He winked as he spoke.

Ronan, my dad, Joe, and Danny had set up the marquee. They had extracted Gerald numerous times until it was decided he was to stay in the stables, then they had arranged tables and chairs seventy times until Joe was completely satisfied, so Ronan grumbled, and then had headed to the pub to drink beer.

I'd had the pleasure of my mother fussing over my hair because she didn't like the cut, and then going through my makeup throwing out anything she thought was old and would pollute me. Maggie frantically recovered all my items from the bin and snuck them back to my room for me.

"You'd think, since this isn't our first rodeo, the grown-ups would just chill out," I said, laughing at the thought of the 'grown-ups.'

I honestly believed my parents, Joe and Danny even, were making things way more complicated than necessary. It was meant to be a simple and small wedding, although I had to take some responsibility for its growth. All the way through the past couple of days, though, my focus had been on Ronan. He hadn't smiled or laughed as much in a long time. He was so happy and no matter what went wrong, he smiled his way through fixing it. There wasn't a thing he couldn't do.

"I can't wait for tomorrow," he said, sliding into bed beside me.

"Neither can I. Technically, you're supposed to be in a different bedroom tonight, did you know that?"

He huffed. "If we were following tradition, I'd have to wear a suit and not the kilt with the work boots and T-shirt you're so desperate to see me in."

I turned to face him and laughed. "You're not?"

He didn't answer me. I couldn't care less what he wore as long as there was at least a kilt involved.

"Are you going to be naked underneath?" I asked. Again, he didn't answer but tapped the side of his nose. "I might be as well then," I added.

"After the official bit, there's a little time to come back here and…rest up, isn't there?" he asked.

"I'm sure there will be. Why, what do you propose?" I teased.

"Well, you show me yours and I'll show you mine," he answered.

"How about we do that now? Just in case it's too busy tomorrow," I offered.

Ronan hummed and then rubbed his chin in mock concentration. "I'm not sure that's the right thing to do. We're not supposed to be in the same bed."

I ignored his comment and launched myself at him. While trying to untangle the sheet that I'd got caught up in and laughing, he wrapped his arms around me and kissed my nose.

"I love you so much," he said before he reached over to his bedside table. He pulled a familiar box from the drawer. "You, naked, but dripping in diamonds is all I want to see right now," he said.

I sat up and allowed him to place the family necklace he'd given me around my neck. I was conscious of breaking it, of course, but Ronan encouraged me to roll to my back and he made love to me, slowly, gently, and with every part of his soul.

5

I woke in an empty bed to crashing and banging coming from downstairs. Ronan had obviously gotten up way earlier than normal. I stretched planning a nice shower and hair wash, a little pampering and some tea before getting ready.

The house had other ideas.

Maggie burst into the bedroom. "No hot water, anywhere," she said, waving one arm wildly while holding a cup of tea in the other.

"Okay, do we know why?" I asked, sitting up in bed.

"Nope, everyone appears to be a boiler expert and is outside in the shed and your mum has her head in the Aga."

"Thankfully, the Aga doesn't run on gas," I said.

Maggie laughed as she placed the tea on the side table. "I did tell her that, she didn't seem to understand me." She then placed her hand on the side of my face. "Today is going to be a wonderful day. The sun is shining, it's going to stay dry all day, and we have a wedding in the garden!" She clapped her hands and rushed out of the room.

I'd just taken a breath and a sip of tea before Joe burst in. "We have no hot—"

"I know," I said.

"How are we going to get ready?" he asked, mortified and with wide eyes.

"Wash from the sink, I guess. It's not the end of the world, Joe, and a regular occurrence up here."

He pouted. "I wanted to style your hair."

"I'm perfectly able to style my own hair. Now, if you don't mind I'd like to get up, and I have no clothes on under this duvet."

"Oh, get you," he said, laughing and then leaving the room. Before he'd managed to shut the door my mother bustled in.

"We have—"

"I know!" I sighed and then rolled my eyes so hard they ached.

"Don't be petulant. I was only telling you. Now, what is the plan for this morning?" she asked, as she sat on the bed and smiled at me.

"I'm going to get up, have a wash, something to eat, then relax for an hour or so before I get ready. You can bring my clothes in here if you want. Ronan is using another room to dress in."

Giving my mother something to do was the only way I could get her out of my bedroom and, even though she was my mother, I wasn't about to stand naked in front of her. She had a habit of commenting on my *untidy bits* or my *little paunch going on there*. She thought she was doing me a good turn to point out my flaws. I wasn't so keen on her good turns.

While she was out of the room, I dashed to the bathroom for a strip wash. I was wrapped in a robe and back in the bedroom when she returned.

"I had to hide so Ronan didn't see your dress," she said, puffing as if she'd run around the house.

"Aw, we're not that worried about all that stuff," I said, taking it from her and hanging it on the front of the wardrobe.

"You should be, it's nice to follow tradition," she mumbled, smoothing down the front of the material.

"I did that once before, look where it got me," I replied, removing her hand from the fabric so she didn't keep stroking it.

"Do you speak with him?"

I was surprised by her question. "No, not since the last solicitor's meeting."

"That's a shame, you have a lot of history together."

I stared at her. I frowned, waiting to see if she would retract her comment. It occurred to me we hadn't been in each other's company for such a long time, I'd forgotten what it was that kept me from visiting as often as I was invited. My mother was often inappropriate but not in her swinging ways. She had always sided with Harry. When I told her about his *coming out,* I remember her telling me I should just stick with him. Let him have his flings but keep a *decent front* for the sake of his work. Her words had stung.

"Surely you'd rather keep this lifestyle than be single?" she'd said.

I decided not to comment and change the subject.

Dragging myself from the memory I said, "If you're up for making a cup of tea and some toasted buns, I'd love one." I was hoping to have her leave me alone for a little while.

She smiled, oblivious to how her comment had affected me. "Of course, darling. I'll rustle up breakfast. You come down when you're ready."

I sat heavily on the bed and tears filled my eyes but I brushed them away. I wasn't doing that. I wasn't going to let my emotions turn the slightest thing negative.

"Bloody menopause," I said, and then laughed. I reached over and picked up the little blue applicator on the bedside cabinet. It was meant to be used that evening but it was going in the drawer for another time. "And you're not doing your job, either."

"Who are you talking you?" Maggie asked, as she walked into the room.

"No one. Myself. God knows," I replied. "I sent my mother downstairs, she was starting to irritate me."

"Yes, thank you. That's why I've come up here," she replied with a laugh. She handed me another cup of tea and we both sat on the bed. "Are you nervous?"

"No, should I be?"

Maggie laughed. "No, of course not. I think Ronan is, though. He's pacing and snapping at everyone outside. Carly told him to go and take a *chill pill*. Is there such a thing? Maybe we could slip one in your mum's tea," she asked.

"I'd have stocked up on those myself if they existed. Although I guess they do, in the form of antidepressants," I said, chuckling. "I do love my parents but she's a bit intense sometimes," I added. Maggie nodded, agreeing with me.

―――

Maggie took a tray of toasted buns out to everyone still setting up. The florist had rigged up the most beautiful display so I had been told. I hadn't wanted to see it until it was done. I wanted that surprise when I walked through the library and out onto the terrace. I could hear them from the opened bedroom window chatting and laughing. I could hear the tinkling of glasses as toasts were being given and I couldn't wait to be down there, joining in.

I heard a soft knock on the bedroom door. "Can I come in?" Ronan asked.

"Hold on," I replied, laughing. I was sitting crossed-legged on the bed in my robe. I jumped up and moved my dress to inside the wardrobe. I didn't do tradition but I didn't want him to see my dress until it was time. "Come in," I called out, settling back on the bed.

He opened the door and then checked the corridor to make sure he wasn't being seen. "Your mum has forbidden me to see you before the ceremony," he said, chuckling.

I patted the bed beside me and he came and sat.

"It sounds like there's a lot going on downstairs," I said.

"It's all done. Looks wonderful, exactly as you wanted." He smiled at me and then snatched a bun from my plate.

"Is that all you wanted from me, my buns?" I asked, wide-eyed and innocently.

"That and your bum. I prefer your bum to your buns I think."

I laughed. "I believe my mum is driving everyone nuts," I said.

"Yeah. But Petal will be here soon so they can get to formally meet each other."

"That's early, isn't it?" We still had a couple of hours before the ceremony.

"We thought it a good distraction," Ronan answered and then winked. "I love your dad, though."

"Are all the animals locked away?"

"For sure. Gerald has got the hump and keeps headbutting the gate between him and Piggy. I see a budding romance going on there."

"At least he's left Bess alone."

"I can't wait to marry you," Ronan said, changing the subject rather abruptly.

"Thank you," I replied, laughing. "Same."

"I'd better go now, I've got to decide what to wear. Charlie has the rings sewn into his pocket and Maggie has to remember to unsew them before midday."

"Why…? No, don't bother." I leaned forwards and kissed him deeply. He tasted of coffee, toasted bun, and Ronan. My nether regions did a little merry dance in anticipation of an evening tasting him again.

When I was on my own I decided to slowly get ready. I washed my hair by leaning over the bath and suffering the cold water—it actually refreshed me and brought down the hot flush I was experiencing—and then dried it. One thing the blooming menopause had taught me was to take things slow. If I rushed in blow-drying my hair, I was a sweaty mess with a mop of frizz similar to Colleen's. Instead, I had the setting on cool and slow and

I took my time. Mum had offered to 'do' my hair but it was fairly short and without any real style, so there wasn't much to do with it. I also had visions of looking like *Annie* with a head of unwanted curls. I was enjoying the peace.

I applied my makeup, and smiled, as it was only one of a handful of times I'd done a full face in the past couple of years. My skin was in great condition, a little tanned and freckled from all the non makeup days out in the fresh air. I tried to straighten out a couple of new wrinkles around my eyes and resorted to one of those fake mascara wands that *guaranteed* longer lashes—I mean, how? Your lashes can only be as long as your lashes are —to open my eyes since my lids had become a little hooded. Within an hour, I was done.

I walked across the room and took out my dress. I placed my new lace shoes on the chair and laid the dress over the bed then checked my watch. Joe had insisted on helping me get dressed, even though I'd told him I'd rather do it on my own. If I had Joe, I told him, I'd have Mum and he was much better at keeping her occupied than I was. I regretted that when I saw the row of buttons at the back I had no hope of doing up alone. I sent him a text.

About ten minutes to midday, come up on your own and help me into this dress, will you? Don't tell Mum

or she'll insist on helping as well, and I can't be doing with her crying all over me.

I placed the phone on the dressing table and gathered my underwear together. A smile started to spread. If Ronan wasn't wearing any undies, neither would I!

I cupped my breasts, thankful they hadn't sagged too much. I could hardly wear a bra but no knickers. If I was going commando, then it was a full on commando. Then I was reminded, my bladder was a bitch. If I needed a pee and I didn't have enough time to get to the loo, I'd have no Tena Lady. I started to fret. I didn't want a Tena Lady in my nice wedding knickers. Unless... I plotted. I'd go commando, then pop on some pants, then go commando again later. There was no way I could dance without any form of *protection* downstairs.

I fretted some more and then wondered what on earth I was fretting about. I was getting married; I was over the moon with that prospect. I was wearing knickers and a slimline Tena and then I'd remove it before... Well, timing would be important, I had all good intentions of Ronan helping me undress as seductively as he could.

———

"Oh my Lord," I said, looking at myself in the mirror. The dress flattered my curves but there was something magical about it.

"You look stunning. Now, your dad is about to come up so make sure you don't cry, okay?" Joe said. He kissed my cheek and left the room giving me a moment to just look.

I reached out and touched the mirror, touching my reflection. The lady who wore this dress originally must have felt like a princess. I certainly did. We'd discovered the dress had been handmade during the war. Material had been sourced from various places and although there was the smallest detail that didn't quite match, whoever had sewn it together had done the most magnificent job. I turned to see the peacock on the back, I was sure I'd have to point out Ronan's name and the flag, it was so subtly done.

There was a slight tap to the door and I called out to come on in. My dad appeared and then covered his mouth. I saw tears form in his eyes and I frowned. This wasn't my first marriage and I was sure he hadn't cried back then.

"You look stunning, my darling," he whispered. I smiled; my words were stuck in my throat.

"Your mother is super pissed she can't walk you down the aisle. According to her, I got to do it once before so it should be her turn." He laughed and I was pleased to see him back to his jovial self.

"Is Ronan downstairs yet?" I asked. I wanted to look out the window and watch.

"He is and he looks dapper," Dad replied. He then held out his arm. "Shall we?"

I smiled and took it, picking up a small bouquet of woodland flowers from my dressing table.

Mum stood at the bottom of the staircase and watched as we descended. She, too, placed her hands over her mouth.

She cocked her head to one side. "You look stunning," she said. I smiled back at her and she added, "I'll tell them you're ready." Then scuttled off.

Dad and I stood outside the library doors and waited until we heard the beginning of the music. The doors were opened and I could see straight through to Ronan with Charlie beside him. I wanted to do the cover of the mouth at that point. I also wanted to cross my thighs to quell the instant throbbing! My man looked like a movie star.

Ronan stood there in his blue family tartan kilt. He had long dark socks and patent shoes. He wore a white dress shirt with a black jacket. The brass buttons glinted as if he'd recently polished them. His sporran ported the same blue tartan in the middle. Charlie was dressed identically.

I smiled broadly and started to walk towards him when he gave me a wink. When I was close enough, he reached out to take my hand. He raised that to his lips and gently kissed my knuckles. Without a word we turned to face the vicar and our ceremony began.

Neither Ronan nor I wanted a religious ceremony. We wanted to skip all the 'blah blah' sections and just concentrate on the important parts. We wanted to be married, we didn't want a lecture on *how to*, God, or all those other things we'd both stood through previous times.

It was short, just as we wanted, and much to everyone's surprise, but soon enough we were signing registers and were officially Mr. and Mrs. Carter-Windford.

While we were having our photo taken I leaned in and whispered, "Do you have anything under that kilt?"

"Nope, you?"

"Sadly, yes. I didn't think it prudent to be commando for the whole day with my bladder."

Ronan laughed and I wondered what people thought we were whispering about.

Once the photographs were done, we were ready to mingle and I gratefully accepted a glass of champagne.

It was during that lull before the afternoon tea was served the animals decided to visit.

6

"Erm, did you let the peacocks out?" Joe asked as he sidled up to me.

I was chatting to Petal and Eric. "No, they still need time to settle in, I think."

He cringed. "Well, I just saw one go past on the back of the goat," he replied.

"On the back of a goat?" Petal asked for clarification and I could understand why. It wasn't every day you heard that statement.

Joe sighed. "Yes. A peacock was riding Gerald." I wasn't sure it was necessary to speak as slowly as Joe had. Petal wasn't deaf.

"Bollocks," I said, and then hastily apologised to Petal who turned sharply to me.

"Let me go and look," she offered. However, I hitched up my skirt and we both left the terrace.

Sure enough, standing on the lawn was Gerald with a peacock on his back. I started to laugh. Gerald stared at me, pleading for help, I was sure. His usually slitty, devil eyes were wide and he stood stock-still, terrified to move, I imagined.

"Oh, should we help him?" Petal asked.

"What's going on?" Maggie said from behind. "I saw you from the terrace and wondered what was happening." She couldn't have, the marquee was in the way but I was happy to have her join us anyway.

I tilted my head. "Did Joe tell you?" I asked. She nodded and tucked her lips inside her teeth to hold back the laughter. I nodded and rolled my eyes. "I want to laugh but look at him," I said.

Gerald bleated at us and it was so pitiful.

"How did the peacock get out?" Maggie asked.

I looked around and caught a fleeting glimpse of cream dash through the woods. "Colleen," I said.

Before we could get any closer, the peacock did the strangest thing. It stamped its foot. Gerald tried to turn his little head enough to look, the peacock stamped again. Gerald was off. The peacock opened its wings and not only did it look magnificent, it was the strangest sight. A peacock riding Gerald as he trotted towards the house.

Towards. The. House.

We darted after them, and the more we ran, or stumbled across the lawn, the faster Gerald ran towards the terrace.

He rounded the marquee before we did and I heard a blood-curdling scream. I came to a screeching halt and Maggie ran into the back of me. I didn't want to look but knew I had to. I slowly walked around the edge of the marquee to see my mother with her arms outstretched, crucifixion style. Ronan was doubled over, and my father stood there with his hands over his mouth. A white smear ran down the front of her coral pink, posh frock. The frock she had told me had taken forever to find, that she'd shown off to all her friends who had practically salivated over it.

Peacock shit, I correctly guessed.

It seemed that, in his panic, Gerald had run circles around her. The peacock had decided to deposit his lunch, although I suspect the buckaroo of a ride had probably loosened his bowels, and the result was that Mother was in the way.

Then, something even stranger happened. Some form of communication occurred between Gerald and the peacock. It was as if the bird had transmitted it had done the naughty to the goat. His devil eyes softened and if a goat could smile, he did. He raised his head proudly and trotted off, quite comfortable at having the bird on his back. If she could, I was sure Colleen was laughing as she hid in the woods.

Joe, in his wisdom, ran forwards and tipped his large glass of white wine over the posh frock. Some hit the shit, most didn't. Mother screamed again.

"Do something," I hissed out as I arrived beside Ronan.

He looked at me with tears streaming down his cheeks. "What? What the fuck can I do?" he said although the words were only just audible, such was his laughter.

"Come on, Mum, let's get you cleaned up," I said, reaching out to take her arm.

"You want to shoot those animals! Look what it did to my frock. And deliberate that was, wasn't it?" She looked around to see if anyone would concur. My father, still with his mouth covered, nodded his head in an obligatory manner. Mum huffed and followed me to the kitchen.

Maggie bustled ahead, and as soon as we entered, she had a bowl of hot water and a sponge to hand. Without trying to touch my mother's privates Maggie gently dabbed.

"Oh, give it here," Mum said, and snatched the sponge from Maggie's hand. She angrily scrubbed at the stain, smearing it further.

"Why don't you put on that nice *afternoon* frock you bought?" I asked. Mum, not wishing to *outdo* the bride, as she'd said, had three outfits for the day and evening.

"I think I'll have to. Can I sue the peacock for the cleaning bill?" she asked. Had it not been my mother I would have laughed, but there was half a chance she was serious.

"Since it's on loan at the moment, I doubt it."

Although not privy to my parents' finances—they were very closed about that kind of thing—I knew they weren't *poor*. She could more than afford the cleaning bill, not that I would let her pay for it anyway. I'd take it into town the following day.

"Well, it wouldn't be the done thing at this place not to have some form of drama, now, would it?" Maggie said, picking up the sponge from where Mum had dropped it.

I started to giggle. "Whose idea were the peacocks?"

Maggie bit her lip and shrugged her shoulders before a squeak managed to escape. "Oh dear, now what do we do?"

"We go and have afternoon tea," I said, brightly. Being shat on by a peacock wasn't the end of the world and in all fairness, probably was a rare event, one Mother could possibly dine out on.

"I meant, what do we do about the animals? They're clearly out and about," Maggie clarified.

"Oh, I'm sure they'll be fine. Come on, it's my wedding day." I took her arm and as we left the kitchen we bumped into Dad.

"Is your mother in there?" he asked, as if there was any other place she could have been.

"She's changing into her afternoon tea dress, I believe," Maggie answered with a smile.

"Ah, okay. I think I'll let her be then. Terribly bad luck to be…well, you know," he said, and there was no hiding the building laugh just waiting to burst out.

"I think it's meant to be good luck," I said.

"Yes, it probably is…to anyone other than your mother. Come on, darling, let's go and get drunk," he said.

The three of us laughed as we rounded the house and headed back to the terrace. I wondered if I should have accompanied my mum to her room and helped her change. I was sure she'd tell me to get back downstairs to the festivities. I hoped she would have, anyway.

"Is everything okay?" Ronan asked, placing his arm around my waist.

"She's getting changed and suing the peacock for her cleaning bill," I replied, smiling up at him.

"You know, it just wouldn't have been right without that lot causing chaos," he said, looking out to the woods in the hopes of catching a glimpse of at least one of the delinquent pets.

"Maggie said the same," I replied with a laugh. "Now, I have an urge to look under your kilt but I think I shall show some restraint. Also, I'm hungry."

Afternoon tea was being laid out on the tables and Joe was encouraging our friends and family to take their seats. In the meantime, a van arrived and Ronan gave a wave to a group of guys who started to unload musical instruments. The band had arrived.

My mother made her grand entrance after we'd all been seated and I exhaled in relief. She curtsied at the French doors with her arms wide, and to applause from our guests. All the time she was the main focal point, she'd be happy. I loved my mother, but her need to be centre of attention irked me at times. She placed her arm around my shoulders and kissed my cheek as she sat.

She sighed, dramatically. "I feel so much better now," she said, waiting for her cup to be filled with tea.

"I'm glad to hear that. I would have hated for you to miss this delicious tea," I replied, and I genuinely meant it. The afternoon tea was magnificent; Maggie had outdone herself with the cakes and sandwiches all laid out on tiered plates.

Our table consisted of my parents, Maggie and Charlie, Angie, since she had been fostered by Maggie and Charlie and therefore viewed as family, and me and Ronan. I would have loved to have had larger tables as, when I looked around, there were so many friends I viewed as family.

Pam and Del were sitting with Jake and being hugely entertained by Petal and Eric. Since the press article about the campers *stumbling* across the naked art group, it had been a topic for conversation every time Pam and I spoke. She was fascinated about the group, to the point of obsession, and I wondered, since they were staying at the campsite, whether we might find them sneaking to see them at some point.

Champagne flowed freely and I winked at Carly as she raised an empty glass to ask a question. I nodded and she poured herself a half glass. I raised mine to her as she sipped. She had a place at a table but was still bustling around. Guests could help themselves if they wanted more bubbles, I had told her. She was part of the family and I wanted her to relax. Ronan and I had plans and had even discussed modernising one of the gatehouses so she could live on site. I turned my attention back to my table. Something had caught my ear.

"So, at her first wedding, she was so anxious she peed herself!" my mother exclaimed, sipping from her fourth, or could have been fifth, glass. I frowned and continued to listen. "Yes, I had to help her change into her evening outfit earlier than necessary."

I looked around the table; Maggie pursed her lips and frowned. Charlie was probably oblivious to what was being said, he was half-cut as it was. Ronan had a fixed grin.

"Mum, I'm not sure that anyone wants to know what happened at my first wedding, let alone that I peed myself, which I don't actually recall," I said.

She screwed up her forehead and cocked her head to one side. "So, if you didn't pee yourself, who did?"

Joe intervened. "Ronan, it must be nice to finally meet Lizzie's mum?" His wide-eyed, *I'm so innocent* look hadn't fooled anyone.

"Wonderful," was all Ronan replied. Mother hiccupped and Dad patted my hand while chuckling, I hoped, at Joe's question.

Ronan reached for my hand, he held it under the table gently letting his thumb run over my knuckles. I didn't need to look at him to know he had probably wanted to laugh at Joe's question as well.

The afternoon wore on. Plates were cleared and more bottles of wine and champagne were brought out. We had decided to lay a series of tables full of ice buckets and guests could help themselves to drink. When it was gone, it was gone. However, seeing the number of boxes and crates Carly and her girls were lugging into the marquee, I highly doubted we'd run out of booze.

I left the table and mingled again. I sat with Pam and Del and we laughed with Jake who had brought his new sweetheart with him. I was pleased to see him with someone, although he had told me he still thought it a shame we never dated. I hoped his partner hadn't heard and that it was the whisky talking!

There were a few minutes when I stood to one side, near the French doors and watched. I loved hearing the laughter and seeing the smiles. I loved watching Ronan chat and take the congratulations given. He would periodically look around as if searching for me, and when he saw me on my own he walked over.

"Are you okay?" he asked, concerned caused his forehead to wrinkle.

"Yes, I'm people watching. I'm having a moment to take it all in, if you know what I mean," I replied. Ronan took both my hands in his and leaned down to kiss me gently on the lips.

He nodded and smiled. "I know what you mean." We stood side by side and watched our family and friends enjoy our special day.

I think that was the last moment of peace. What followed was hilarious, excruciating, and, well…

7

The band had struck up one of their own songs and Ronan and I were encouraged to dance to it. I was flat-footed and he was uncoordinated but we managed to waltz around the dance floor, only knocking into a couple of people. My parents, Maggie and Charlie, and Petal and Eric soon joined us. However, when Petal and Eric started to resemble a couple from *Strictly Come Dancing* we gave way and stood to the side, clapping. They were amazing and for an old girl who used a Zimmer frame most of the time, I was amazed at how easily Eric whizzed her around the dance floor; that was, until I noticed she was standing on his feet. Not to be outshone, of course, my parents decided on a seriously raunchy tango.

I shuddered at the faces my mother pulled. I wasn't sure if she was trying to look erotic or constipated.

Other couples soon joined them, so Ronan and I snuck off to the bar. The marquee was filling up nicely and we weren't getting much time to ourselves. We were constantly being interrupted by guests either commenting on the wedding, the castle, the grounds, or congratulating us. It was nice to see how the locals held Ronan in such high regard.

I wasn't sure what made me look over to the entrance. There wasn't a sound that had me on alert, more a feeling in my gut. Ronan was deep in conversation with one of the students who, a little tipsy, was trying to talk about felling trees. I gently nudged Ronan and then diverted my gaze to the entrance.

Standing there, weaving from side to side was a very obviously drunk Rich. Not only Rich but also a *snidely* looking Gregg. I doubted it was coincidence they had arrived at the same time.

"Wait here," Ronan whispered, dipping his head to my level.

I glanced around to find an ally and my gaze fell on Joe. He frowned, not close enough to know what was going on, but perhaps picking up on my panicked expression. I turned to the entrance, Joe followed suit, and I watched his eyes widen before he rushed over to me.

In the time it took Joe to get to me, chaos ensued.

I had no idea what Rich had said but it had resulted in Ronan pulling his arm back, ready for a punch. Charlie darted to his aid and held onto Ronan's arm. That was until Rich started laughing.

It wasn't Ronan that put Rich on his arse but Charlie. The old boy was so quick, everyone in the marquee had stopped to watch but I believed no one was completely sure what had happened. Although after seeing Charlie punch him, even I stared in disbelief.

It seemed that most of the men gathered around the entrance, and most of the women around me.

I heard the screech of my mother's voice above all the shouting. "Oh my God, this is just awful. A fight at my daughter's wedding! I knew she should have just eloped."

"Oh…shut up, Mother," I said, growling at her in annoyance. I stomped over to the join the men.

It didn't appear Rich was hurt, or if he was, the anaesethic effect of the copious amounts of alcohol enabled him to sit up, rub his jaw, and then laugh.

"Jesus, Charlie, you want to chill. You're too old to start a fight with me," Rich said, scrambling to his feet.

Charlie took a boxer's stance. He widened his feet and raised his fists. He rocked from foot to foot, waving his fists in a circular movement. "Come on now, laddie. I've tanned your arse many a time in the past," Charlie said.

"Gregg, get the fuck out of here and take him with you. Neither of you were invited for this very reason. You don't get to spoil this day," Ronan said, his voice was so low I suspected the local dogs might start howling.

Gregg ignored Ronan's advice, and instead tapped a cigarette from his packet, raised it to his lips, and lit it. He blew the lungful of smoke straight into Ronan's face. That was his undoing.

I covered my mouth but screamed as Ronan leapt at him so fast, there was nothing Charlie or anyone could do. All the years of hurt and hate were expelled through his fists in a mere matter of seconds before Gregg was spread-eagle in the mud.

As if we weren't able to protect ourselves, the helpers arrived.

Colleen rushed over with Gerald by her side. Gerald, as quick as a fly, fell to his front knees, revved his hind legs and pounded into Rich so hard he flew forwards into the entrance of the marquee, not only taking Charlie with him, but a few guests as well.

Goats love to climb. Gerald loved to headbutt *and* climb. With both Charlie and Rich rolling on the hessian matting, Gerald jumped on top, scrambling to stay balanced. He reminded me of the 90's TV show, *Gladiators*, when they fought while balancing on a greasy pole laid out across a pool of water. Petal was waving her scarf, as if trying to distract a bull from a matador but Gerald wasn't having any of it. Once I was able to pull my hands from my mouth, and shut off the screaming I could hear from my mother, I turned my attention back to Ronan. He was standing but Colleen had decided to sit on Gregg. Not just sit on Gregg. She had her fat backside right in his face. He wiggled and pounded on her, but she wasn't moving.

Joe grabbed my arm and I then turned to him. His mouth was making the perfect O. I was sure mine matched but then I started to laugh. Tears formed in my eyes as that laughter built. I held my stomach as my muscles objected to being so forcibly moved to accommodate my body shaking with mirth.

Joe held my arm and laughed as well. "It's like a Western," he screeched. And it was, except instead of *all* the people fighting, it was half the people and a bunch of nutty animals.

When the peacock rushed into the marquee and decided to see what was going on, my mother fainted. Petal stopped shaking her scarf at Gerald—who had jumped off Rich but continued to butt his side and anyone else within range—and instead, she waved it over my mother's face.

"She needs air," Petal shouted. Eric rushed forward with a glass of water. I wasn't sure if he had simply misheard or thought waterboarding Mother would be better when he threw it over her.

I couldn't hear anymore. I was bent over double and soon enough, because laughter is infectious, ripples started around the marquee.

"Baby, are you okay?" I heard. I was still bent over double. I shook my head, unable to speak.

Ronan crouched down so he could see my face. Surprise made him frown hard. "Are you laughing?" His voice raised an octave. I nodded.

He shook his head that time, and I imagined it was in disbelief. I managed to stand and he did the same. Joe was still clinging to my arm and when I turned to him, he laughed harder, pointing at me. I knew, by the sting in my eyes I must have had mascara dripping down my face.

"I don't…" Ronan started but tailed off.

"That has got to be the funniest…" I hiccupped out the words. "…funniest thing I've seen in ages. And I've peed a little."

Although Ronan laughed, I thought it was more in shock, or because, as I'd said, laughter was infectious.

"Look," I spluttered and pointed to Colleen still sitting on Gregg's head. She was looking our way, chewing a mouthful of grass as if she didn't have a care in the world. If she had shoulders, she would have shrugged them. She batted her long lashes at us and I wanted to kiss her. More so when, with a loud fart, she slowly stood allowing Gregg, who was heaving, to roll away.

All the way through the fighting, the band continued to play folk songs that were, inexplicably, at the same tempo as the boxing, weaving, rolling around, staggering, laughing fighters. It was like a soundtrack to a ridiculous and bizarre movie sequence.

By the time most of the commotion was over, Piggy rolled up. My mother was finally sitting in a chair dabbing at the tears I was sure were fake. She gripped my father's hand, wailing at how awful the day had turned out. Piggy decided to comfort her. He strolled over and rested against her legs. Except, he weighed a few hundred pounds and my mother was sitting on an unstable chair on hessian matting. She and the chair went over, startling poor Piggy who shit in fright.

For the second time that day one of my pets had shit on my mother's posh frock.

I was incapable of helping her that time. She screamed at the animal, which angered Charlie, who grabbed poor Piggy by the ear and towed him away. Colleen sauntered around the marquee relieving people of their sausage rolls, and Gerald stood like a pint-sized bull, all puffed up and aggressively challenging anyone who wanted to tackle him and his pool noodle covered horns. The peacock just upped his tail feathers as if flipping us all the bird and went off to find his partner.

My mother rushed past, still wailing, with my father in tow. By the time they got to the castle, the police had arrived.

"Who called the police?" I asked.

"Fuck knows. Wait here, let me sort it," Ronan said. He strode off with Charlie, who still had hold of Piggy's ear, to placate the police.

"Well... Well, what a party," Joe said.

"I know, honestly, it was like watching a movie!"

Joe put his arm around my shoulders. "This is most certainly one for the history books."

Danny came over, and also placed his arm around my shoulders from the other side. "I think we'll dine out on this for years to come."

I looked around the marquee to see a couple of men getting up from the floor and one woman dabbing the front of her dress, trying to soak up the drink that had been spilled over her. Some people were still laughing; some re-enacting Charlie's boxer stance, and other's were preparing to leave. I guessed the reception, for them, was over.

The police called Gregg and Rich to one side and it wasn't long before Ronan returned and the police had ordered both Gregg and Rich from the property. No charges were going to be brought, thankfully, but I was still curious to know who had called the police. That was until Ronan received a text message.

I'm sorry. I told Gregg about your wedding, and he told Rich to wind him up in the hopes he'd spoil it. I wish you and Lizzie well, Ronan, and I'm sorry if I caused any trouble. I called the police when I heard shouting. I hope I didn't do wrong. Carol.

"Carol?" I asked as he finished reading the text. He turned the phone so I could read for myself.

"What a bitch," he said.

"No, I don't think so. Look, she wishes us well and I don't think for one minute she thought there would be a fight."

"Yet she was close enough to hear a commotion and call the police, Lizzie. That means she's here. She probably came with them!"

"What a bitch!" I replied.

We both stomped from the marquee to see if we could find her. Colleen trotted beside and I placed my hand on her neck. If Carol had been outside, she was long gone by that point. What we did see, however, was my dad loading suitcases into the boot of Joe's car. Joe and Danny were standing beside the car and Joe shrugged his shoulders when he saw me.

"Your mother wants to find a local hotel, she's adamant," Dad said, apologetically.

"Why? Just because an animal shit on her dress?" I asked, surprised by that turn of events. I expected my mother to be upset but not punish us by leaving.

Dad just sighed. Mother left the house and marched over. "Don't try to stop me, Elizabeth. I don't think I feel safe staying here. I'm in fear of my life. My life, Lizzie!" Before anyone could respond, she climbed into the rear seat of the car and slammed the door.

"Oh well," I said, smiling at Ronan.

"I'm so sorry, Ronan, Lizzie," Dad said, and he genuinely meant it.

"Take her to the pub, they have rooms, I'll call ahead," Ronan said, as he stepped away and raised his phone to his ear.

I gave my dad a tight hug and he kissed my cheeks. "Best wedding I've been to in years," he whispered before joining his wife.

The car manoeuvred down the drive and Mum didn't look back once.

"Are you okay?" Ronan asked.

"Sure. It's her choice. I think I probably forgot the reasons why we get on well when we're not in the same country." I meant what I said, although it was said with a slight pang of hurt. "Anyway, we still have some guests, beer, and a band!"

I took his hand and led him back to the marquee. A cheer rose up as we entered and we started our wedding reception from scratch. We danced our first dance to a different tune.

"It wouldn't be the same if we didn't have to do everything three times, would it?" I said, and then we laughed. The music changed and he and Charlie strutted around, all Mick Jagger style, to the raucous laughter of our friends, the ones who were left, anyway. Dancing clearly wasn't Ronan's thing but looking bloody sexy with a kilt flying around was. He'd lost the jacket and rolled up his shirtsleeves, and it wasn't much later that I got to see what he wore under his kilt.

The band had been playing some traditional folk songs and while I, and others, stood in a semi-circle and clapped, the Scottish men did their thing. As badly as they could—and I thought that might be deliberate—they jigged around. When the song came to an end, they all turned their backs, bent at the waist and lifted their kilts to show us a row of bare bums. So it was true, not one of them worn underpants! And that included Charlie who didn't have the same foresight of the other men, which was to hold their cock and balls. Instead, his dangled down and I was reminded of Limp Dick. In fact, Petal screamed with laughter the loudest while looking at me, I knew she just had the same thought in mind.

"I don't have enough bleach for my eyes," Joe wailed, covering them as if that would erase the sight.

When the kilts were released and the boys turned back to face their audience, Charlie was grinning like a Cheshire cat, toothless, but happy as anything. Ronan wrapped me in his arms.

"See, commando," he said, proudly.

"Always?" I asked.

He winked at me and half smiled. "Now that would be telling."

The rest of the evening blurred. We drank too much, ate too much, and danced until I was barefoot and tripping over my train. I hadn't bothered to change into my reception attire, it seemed too much effort, but I was conscious of the dress getting too dirty. At some point, and I had no idea of the time, Ronan scooped me up in his arms and I was carried, officially, over the threshold. He placed me down once we were inside the hall.

"Welcome home, Mrs. Carter-Windford," he said, quietly.

I smiled at him. He lifted my hand and kissed my wedding and engagement rings, the original one that matched the necklace I'd been forever checking was still around my neck that day.

"Thank you, Mr. Carter-Windford," I replied. "I do think you need to carry me to bed."

"That sounds like a great invitation."

"More so because, my eyes are squiffy and I'm not sure I'll manage the stairs on my own," I replied with a laugh.

He did just that and while he carried me up, we could hear the laughter of guests finally leaving and the clanking as the band packed up their instruments.

"Who's in charge down there?" I enquired, worried about the gate being open and errant animals.

"Joe. Well, Danny since he's teetotal and Joe is as pissed as a fart," he replied. He huffed and shifted me up his body a little.

"I'm not heavy, am I?" I asked.

Ronan kicked open the bedroom door. "No," he said as he unceromoniously dumped me on the bed. "But you wiggle too much."

"Oh, I wanted you to undress me." I pouted as I spoke.

"Do you think you could stand?" he asked, pulling his shirt over his head, kicking off his shoes and rolling off his socks.

I licked my lips and stared at his abs. He clicked his fingers to gain my attention.

"Huh?" I said.

"Do you think you can stand?" he asked, again.

"Probably not." Even I was aware of the slur in my voice. Then I chuckled.

Ronan climbed on the bed just in his kilt and rolled me to my front. "I'll undress you here," he said.

I lay still, loving the slowness of his touch and smiling. When prompted, I raised slightly so he could slip the dress forwards and off my shoulders. I rose further as he pulled it down my body. When it was off, I rolled to my back.

"Now that is a beautiful sight," he whispered.

I was laying in just my knickers and stockings. As he slid his hands down my sides, his tongue trailing down my stomach, I shot up so fast, I bumped into his head.

"What the...?" he said.

"Ouch," I said at the same time. "You can't go there. I need the bathroom. Girl's things," I stammered through my statement.

Ronan laughed. "Lizzie if you mean you've got a panty pad thing there, I know, I can see it. I'm not about to feast on it, so don't worry."

I gasped. "How do you know about panty pads?"

"When I was a kid, Maggie used to have the largest panty pad things on the planet. She'd stick them to the soles of our feet and tell us to pretend to ice skate around the hall." Ronan started to laugh at the memory; I just frowned in shock at him. "Anyway, little did we know, she was just getting us to polish the floor!"

I gasped some more. Not only did I gasp, I could feel my cheeks heating from shock. My eyebrows couldn't physically raise any further, even if I'd tried. Ronan really started to laugh then. He pushed me back on the bed, quickly stripped my knickers down, all the while I wiped the tears of laughter from my cheeks.

"What do you do normally?" he asked, resting on his hands above me.

"Get to the bathroom before you get all…amorous," I said.

"Well, the ice skate has gone now. I'm assuming it's not hooha happy pill day as well, is it?"

I reached up and grabbed both sides of his head. As he laughed, I pulled him down to me. It was lovely to kiss him hard while he tried to contain his laughter. Soon, however, he wasn't laughing anymore.

8

The sun was shining through the open curtains, and I knew I was alone in the bed. I turned on my side to look out the window and wonder if, at any second, a banging headache or nausea would come. I smiled and nodded to myself when neither did. Perhaps sticking to champagne all night was the cure for hangovers.

I felt my necklace twist around my neck and I was worried because I'd slept in it all night. I gently took it off and placed it back in the box. It would have to live in the safe until such an occasion warranted it being worn again. I looked at it before I closed the lid. The Mountford Diamond, I recalled Ronan telling me. There was a book in the library written by the relative who had owned that diamond and I was determined to find it and learn more. I gently pushed back the duvet and, gingerly,

I slipped my legs over the side of the bed and sat up. Still no hangover.

"Mmm," I said, to myself and I gave it a minute before I stood.

I was in desperate need of a bath or shower, I smelled of sex and alcohol and when I surveyed the room, seeing clothes strewn all over the floor, I laughed. I guessed I needed to tidy up as well. Bending down to pick up my dress wasn't an option. I tried, but then wobbled; perhaps I wasn't as steady on my feet as I'd thought. I headed to the bathroom instead. While I was in the shower, I heard Ronan shout he had a mug of tea for me.

When I returned, wrapped in a towel, he was sitting on the bed, having made it and picked up all the clothes from the floor.

"How's the head?" he asked.

"Surprisingly good. Was I very drunk?" I asked.

"Mildly," he replied with a laugh. He handed me my tea and I gratefully sipped.

I sat beside him. "How are you?" I asked. I picked up his hand to inspect his knuckles.

"I'm grand, Charlie, not so." He chuckled when he spoke. "He has a black eye that he's insisting had nothing to do with him rolling on the floor with Rich."

"Oh gawd. I can't believe there was a fight at our wedding," I said, joining him in amusement. "And my mother!" Memories of her storming off flooded back.

For the second time, Ronan and I convulsed with laughter. "I don't think she'll come and say goodbye before she leaves, will she?" I asked, knowing the answer.

"We can go and see them if you like?" Ronan suggested.

"No, honestly. I think I've lied to myself about our relationship for years. We've never really got on. She's just too dramatic for me sometimes." I laughed again, but this time it was tinged with a little sadness at the admission.

We both heard a groan from outside the bedroom. It was followed by a gentle knock.

"Come in," Ronan said. I frowned at him; I was still wrapped in a towel.

Joe walked through the door carrying a brown paper-wrapped parcel. He pointed to the window and groaned again before placing the parcel on the bed.

"Are we meant to understand what that means?" I asked, holding back a giggle. I don't think I'd ever seen Joe so dishevelled. He groaned and pointed again. It was only the squint that gave away what he wanted to communicate.

"Close the curtains, I think," Ronan said, and Joe nodded.

"Go close the curtains in your own bedroom," I scolded, proudly showing him I was *hangoverless*. He snarled at me. I pointed to the parcel. "And what is this?"

He just shrugged his shoulders then flopped onto a chair in the corner. "Did we all have a fight last night?" he asked, keeping his eyes closed.

Ronan snorted. "No, we *all* didn't. If I recall, you and Lizzie stood laughing like hyenas while the rest of us had a fight. That was until the animals came to our rescue, oh, and then the police. And then, you drove Lizzie's parents to the pub while bladdered!"

"While drunk?" I asked, turning sharply to Ronan.

Ronan gestured at Joe. "Well, he wasn't sober, was he?"

I stared at Joe who simply shrugged his shoulders. "I have no idea what I did."

"You're lucky there isn't any local police," I scolded.

Joe started to laugh. "Danny drove, not me, Miss Moral…something." He shook his head, not knowing what word to add to the insult. "He pushed me out of the way and got in the driver's seat. You were there. What a party, huh? I wonder who has black eyes this morning?"

"Well, Charlie, for one," I replied, and then chuckled. "Now, if you don't mind, I'd like to get dressed."

He didn't move, just waved his arm as if giving me permission to do so. In fairness, I had dressed in front of him before.

"I think that's code for she wants to jump my bones," Ronan said. Only then did Joe colour and leave the bedroom rather quicker than he had arrived.

"As much as I'd love to jump your bones, I'm not sure I'm coordinated enough and I'm not sure my stomach would hold up with too much movement. I'm happy to just lay like a limpet while you get on with it, of course," I said, smirking at him.

"I've remembered, this is a gift from the film crew," I said, picking up the parcel. On his nod, I tore off the wrapping. Inside was a framed still of the front of the castle, the cars lined the drive and the actors were walking to the door carrying their vintage suitcases.

"Oh my Lord," I said.

"It's brilliant. That will go nicely in the office, and on the website," Ronan added. I nodded in agreement. It might entice more location scouts to check us out.

Once I placed the photograph back on the bed, I stood.

Ronan slapped my backside. "Come on, let's get some food in your stomach and see if that settles it. After all the activity last night, I think it might be my turn to lay like a limpet," Ronan replied. He kissed my temple and rose from the bed.

I dragged on some underwear, jeans, and a T-shirt. I fiddled around trying to get the flip-flops onto my feet and the toe-bar between my toes, and then followed him downstairs.

The kitchen was a hub of laughter. Maggie was in her element and it looked like she was cooking for the five thousand. Pam and Del were there, Jake and his partner, and Charlie was regaling them, again, of the evening events, even though they were there at the time. Joe and Danny sat on the kitchen countertop, and even Petal was cooking up a storm on the Aga.

"Where's Eric?" I asked, snatching a piece of sausage from her pan.

"Gone for a walk, he needs the fresh air before he can eat," she replied, slapping my hand away.

"Right, everyone to the terrace," Maggie shouted. I raised my eyebrows at Ronan, who shrugged his shoulders in return.

As we approached, it was clear most of our guests had returned for a wedding breakfast; only one that took place *after* the event. Carly was filling glasses with champagne and although one was thrust into my hand, I wasn't sure I could drink it. I topped it up with orange juice from the jug on the table.

Each table had been laid for breakfast and I wondered when Maggie had done that. Someone, in their wisdom, played the *Rocky* soundtrack as Charlie walked through the door, and he bounced around on his tiptoes shadow-boxing. I shook my head and laughed.

It was blooming amazing and the perfect antidote to my mildly unsettled constitution.

While we tucked into sausages and eggs, talk was of the evening before. For those who had encountered our pets for the first time, they were desperate for another meeting. I promised a tour of the grounds once we'd eaten. I had every confidence that Piggy, Colleen, and Gerald would be safe and wandering around somewhere but I wasn't sure about the peacocks. I hated the thought I might look in the lane and see one squashed.

"Did you see the way the peacock stood on Gerald's back?" Maggie asked, reminding us of the unfortunate incident when it *destroyed* my mother's dress.

"That was so odd," I replied, laughing at the memory. "Maybe that might be a budding friendship and he can leave Bess alone."

I looked around at the tables and our guests. It seemed our misfit of animals were in great company with our misfit of friends. Londoners mixed with Kentish Men—who were apparently different to Men of Kent, or so I was constantly told when I moved there—they mixed with Scots, and none of them could understand the other. Partly, it was because most were still hungover, and partly because, when hungover, I noticed the Scots' accent was much heavier. However, the universal language of laughter was abundant.

With breakfast over, it was time to, firstly, feed the peafowl. I'd learned, as part of my research before approaching the rescue charity, that peafowl, like cats, would decamp to a neighbour if the food was better. I was determined to keep them free roaming but wanting to stay. Ronan had agreed to make some platforms among the branches of trees so they could stay off the ground if predators arrived and it would also be a handy place to put feed.

With a bucket in one hand, Pam, Del, Jake, and Delia—I finally got to learn her name—accompanied Joe and me on the feeding round. Danny and Ronan were staying behind to dismantle the marquee and stack away most of the tables and chairs from the terrace.

"Do they bite?" Pam asked, as we scanned for the birds.

"The males can be aggressive, and they fuck up your cars because they think the reflection is another male," Jake answered. I was impressed with his knowledge.

"Sounds like a lovely pet," Joe added.

"They're not really pets but it would be nice if we could get close enough to stroke them," I said.

The scream the peacock made wasn't the most pleasant of sounds, especially after a boozy night, but gave us an indication of which direction to take. Before we entered the woodland to the side of the castle, I started to leave piles of food. I'd need to be sure that Piggy, Colleen, and Gerald didn't wolf it all down, they would eat anything!

"There they are," Joe said, pointing.

The peacock was displaying and he looked magnificent. His tail feathers were held high and if I were a peahen, I'd surely be impressed. I clucked my tongue, not having a clue what noise to make to tempt them and we stood still. Both birds walked slowly towards us. According to the rescue centre they had been bred in captivity but kept in a pen way too small in a suburban house. The neighbours had complained so much about the noise, the mess, and the damage to vehicles that the owners, rightly so, had decided they needed a better and larger home. Our grounds were just perfect for them; all we had to do was make sure they stayed. I was concerned; they hadn't experienced this much space before. I didn't want them to wander too far to begin with.

"Can't we put butter on their feet?" Joe asked. We all frowned at him in confusion. "Like you do to cats," he explained. We all turned to him and our brows furrowed with confusion. "You put butter on cat's feet so they leave a trail, don't you?"

"I highly doubt it and you'd never get close enough to put butter on its feet," Jake added.

"They are lovely, we should get some for the village," Delia said, clinging to Jake's arm possessively.

I couldn't say whether I'd taken to her or not. She wasn't forthcoming in conversation yet I wasn't sure that was necessarily shyness. She just didn't seem to want to mix, which was a shame.

While we stood and contemplated names for the peafowl, the peahen decided to come and investigate. She seemed the tamer of the two, and the less naughty, I thought, hopefully. She reached out and pecked some seed from my hand. That was until her mate decided he was rather jealous and strutted over. He barged her out of the way and snatched the largest mouthful of seed he could. It seemed we had discovered, outside of their pen, their sleeping quarters. A patch of ground had been scratched and it looked like a little nest had been made. I wondered if we might see eggs.

"Erm, what's that?" Joe asked pointing to the nest. I peered, not wishing to get too close for fear of angering the peacock. He was already territorial.

"I can't see what you're pointing at," I said.

"I can see something shiny," Del said. He strode forward and came to a full stop when the peacock screamed at him. "It's a watch."

"A watch?" I asked.

"Yes, looks like a silver watch in the nest."

"Do peacocks steal shiny things? I know magpies do," I said. "I'll distract him, you grab the watch."

I started to lay a trail of food and thankfully, the greedy little sod was soon following me. That allowed Del to rush forward and grab the watch. He popped it in his pocket until we were safely back at the terrace.

"Whose is it?" I asked. It certainly wasn't Ronan's.

"No idea. No one has mentioned losing a watch, have they?" Joe asked. I shrugged my shoulders.

I picked it up and studied it. It was a nice piece, clean, which led me to believe it hadn't been found in the grounds.

"Someone must have taken it off last night and he pinched it," Pam said.

"Great, just what we need, a thieving peacock to add to the reprobates," I said, and then laughed. I'd keep the watch in the kitchen and I was sure someone might call or message asking if we'd found one.

It was later that evening, when the marquee had been taken down and the area cleaned up that I remembered the watch. Maggie, Charlie, Ronan and I, Joe and Danny were sitting in the kitchen.

I fished around in my pocket for the watch and placed it on the table. "We found this today in a nest the peacock had made."

Ronan picked it up. "It's not mine," he said. I told him I didn't think it was. "Seems too clean to have been found outside so I wonder if it was one of our guests."

"That's what I thought. Has anyone mentioned a lost watch?" I asked.

"Not that I'm aware of," he said.

We left it on the table and decided to send an email to our guest list and ask if anyone was missing a watch. Pam and Del, Jake and Delia had left that afternoon but I knew a few guests were still at the hotel.

"What are your plans tomorrow?" I asked Joe. I knew they would be leaving the following day.

"We're going to leave in the morning and then head to Danny's parents' for a couple of days," he replied.

I hadn't had the pleasure of meeting Danny's parents despite inviting them to the wedding. It seemed they were a rather unassuming couple, although lovely according to Joe, and felt awkward meeting me for the first time at my wedding. I understood, and said we'd make plans for later in the year when the summer holiday activity had eased off a little.

The following morning, we waved off Joe and Danny and made promises to 'pop down' to Kent for a long weekend. I decided to show Ronan where I'd found the watch. I was still a little perplexed as to how it came to be with the peafowl.

"There's something else there," he said as we approached the scratched earth that we'd seen the penhen sitting in.

That time there was a bangle. A silver bangle that looked well worn. Both the peacock and penhen were off on their wanders so we managed to pick it up without any problems. It was quite small, probably a teen or child's bracelet.

"Where on earth are they getting these from?" I asked. As I looked up at Ronan and saw him looking to the distance, something dawned on me. "You don't think…?"

"I do think. We've got ourselves our own Bonnie and Clyde."

I started to laugh, not that it was funny, of course. What with Ronnie and Reggie, the chickens, the last thing we needed was to add to our misfits with more master criminals. Ronan was looking down towards the camping area.

"Let me go and get the watch and we'll take a drive down," I said. We raced back to the house. I grabbed the watch and then joined Ronan in the courtyard as he started one of the quads.

"What if you're right?" I asked as I climbed on board.

"We might have to rethink the peacock idea," he replied.

I hoped we were wrong and that one of the birds hadn't been on a burglary mission of tents and caravans. They'd only been with us a few days but I was already fond of them. We drove down to the campsite office.

"Morning, how's your head…and fists?" Angie asked as we entered.

"Both good," Ronan replied and then laughed.

"We've found some jewellery. A—"

"A watch?" Angie asked, a hopeful look crossed her face.

"Yes, how did you know?"

"A gentleman asked if I could put a little note up. He's not sure where he lost it, though."

"Mmm, well, it might be that we have a problem. I also have a bangle." I placed the items on the counter that separated us.

"Oh that's pretty. Looks like a child's one," she said, holding up the bracelet.

"Bonnie and Clyde have taken a shine to…shiny things," Ronan said. I rolled my eyes at him.

"Bonnie and…?" Angie enquired.

"The peafowl. We found these in a nest they'd made. Have you seen them down this far?" I asked.

"Yeah, all the time. They like hanging around the loch. The visitors love them. I meant to call you today and tell you," Angie answered.

"They'll have to go," Ronan said, crossing his arms to emphasise that he was serious.

"NO!" both Angie and I said at the same time.

"We can't get rid of them. If we know this is happening, we can add a note to the welcome pack for people to keep their belongings with them at all times," I said, nodding as I did, agreeing with myself.

"And how many claims of Rolexes going missing do you think we'll get?" Ronan asked, tightening his crossed arms.

"Okay, so we don't put that in the welcome pack. But if we know where items are likely to end up, it won't be hard to hand them back, will it? And maybe it's just a settling in phase," I said with a pleading tone.

"It might be a one…a two-off thing," Angie added, backing me up.

"If it happens a lot, Lizzie, we're going to have to reconsider. We can't have guests complaining our bloody birds have stolen things all the time," Ronan said, uncrossing his arms.

I knew he was correct, of course, but I wanted to give the birds just a little time to settle in and hoped it wasn't something they'd get used to doing.

"We could put things in the woods, shiny things. Tie them to trees or, whatever. You've got to make them some platforms so they can get off the ground, we can add things there. It might keep them in the woods," I said, my speech getting quicker with each word because I was excited by the idea.

"We can try that, but I'm serious on this one. We can't have them stealing things. One chance, then we'll reconsider, deal?" Ronan said.

Angie and I nodded. "Anyone got any CDs?" I asked. All shook their heads.

"You'd probably get a couple of cheap ones in town. I'll look this afternoon," Angie offered.

If we could dot shiny things around where we'd rather the peafowl lived, it might entice them to stay there. As we'd discovered, they weren't the most hygienic of animals, we didn't want them shitting everywhere around the campsite either.

"I want to call in on Petal, is that okay?" I said to Ronan, and I climbed behind him on the squad.

"Sure, I'll drop you off and you can walk back if you like. I'm not comfortable there," he said with a chuckle. I gripped him around the waist as he took off.

Petal was in charge of the naked art group and since the publicity we'd recently received, the interest in the group was keeping her busy. I'd offered to help but, having been a secretary in the past—so she kept telling me—she was more than capable.

Ronan came to a halt and I kissed the back of his head. He laughed as I climbed off and gave me a wave over his shoulder. I took the path that led to the art group's private area. As I walked I saw someone and only from behind. But they looked familiar. I recognised the haircut.

"Oh no," I said, probably too loudly as it caused the man ahead of me to turn.

"Darling, how lovely to see you," my dad said.

I covered my eyes quickly. "Dad! I thought you'd left already," I said.

"Oh no, your mum wanted a couple of days doing art. Didn't she tell you?" He did seem a little perplexed when he'd asked. Obviously, I couldn't see him but the hesitancy in his voice had me worried a little.

"No, clearly not. Is she here as well?" I asked. I had no desire to see my mother naked any more than I wanted to see my dad in the same state.

"Oh yes, her and…I forget his name, are painting the… landscape." Dad chuckled as he spoke, and I wondered if Big Cock had her painting him again.

"I think I know what you mean. Will you join us for lunch or dinner?" I asked, still with my hands over my eyes.

"I'll ask your mother. She doesn't want her life at risk with your animals," he said, laughing at the thought.

"The animals live on the grounds, so she's more likely to encounter one here than in the house. Tell her to stop being so silly and to call me. I presume you've got your phones on you?"

"Where would we put them? We don't have pockets, Lizzie." Dad laughed yet again.

That time I chuckled along. "Okay, but get Petal to call me then."

"Were you coming to the camp?" Dad asked.

"I was, but I just remembered somewhere else I'm meant to be." It was a cop out and it wasn't about not seeing my mother after her tantrum, but not seeing them both naked if I could help it.

I turned and walked away, shouting over my shoulder for one to call me about meeting up. I also added, if they didn't have the time—and I sort of hoped they didn't—then to at least let us run them to the ferry.

"Will do," Dad called out, and his voice was so jolly that it actually pricked my heart. He was a lovely man and I wondered why he didn't stand up to my mother sometimes.

I sighed and walked. A rustling in the bushes beside me had my heart, initially, racing until I saw Colleen.

"Hello, you," I said, clucking my tongue at her. She walked beside me and I placed my hand on her neck. "You always turn up at the right time. I wonder who you were in a previous life." Gerald raced from the woods, presumably having only just realised Colleen had left, and I wondered where Piggy was. "All right, we weren't ignoring you," I said to Gerald, as he butted the back of my legs.

The three of us made our way back to the courtyard. Ronan was in one of the sheds with a piece of machinery, a log towing thingy, in pieces. He'd hook the machine up to the back of a quad when they felled trees and it would drag it all the way back.

"Guess what?" I asked as I approached.

"You saw your dad naked in the woods?" he asked, looking at me all innocent and with earnest.

"How did you know that?" I asked, disappointed I couldn't shock him with the news.

"He called me," Ronan replied, laughing. "They can't make dinner because apparently your mum is teaching meditation to the group this evening. However, they would appreciate the lift to the ferry in the morning. She'll call you to make arrangements."

I snorted in response. "Will she now?"

Ronan stood. "Baby, come on. You know your mother. She has to make a statement. She'll be back when she wants a holiday, don't you worry."

I knew he was correct, of course, but it seemed rather extreme to ignore us when all that had happened was a couple of animals pooped on her dresses. There had to be more to it, I thought. Anyway, I wasn't going to stress over it any longer. We had a business to run and we hadn't thought about when to sneak off for a honeymoon. We'd booked out Christine because we thought it might be fun but then other estate matters seemed to rear their heads.

"Want to get away for a couple of days?" he asked, as if reading my mind.

"We can't. We've got the film crew back tomorrow and God knows what's going to happen with Bonnie and Clyde and all that metal lying around."

"Bonnie and Clyde!" Ronan repeated, laughing. "I hadn't meant that to be their names but it does suit them. We'll make sure Charlie checks the nest every day and we'll let the crew know. I've got nothing I can't do later in the week, neither have you. And it might be the kick your mother needs to know you've gone away without saying goodbye."

"I said we'd take them to the ferry," I replied, weakly because Ronan's idea was growing on me

"Charlie can do that."

I looked up at him and smiled. He smiled back down to me. "Okay. Go and get Christine and I'll pack some things together."

Christine's holiday crockery and cutlery wasn't the same as the personal stuff I had stashed away in a box. Not that it was better, just prettier. It would take half an hour to change the bed, replace the towels and other items, to make it feel like it was ours alone, and while Ronan walked over to the office to get a set of Land Rover keys, I rushed inside.

"Where's the fire?" Maggie called out.

"We're going to take Christine for a honeymoon," I said, excitedly.

"That's all last minute, isn't it?" she replied.

"I know, but we've got a couple of days, according to Ronan, so we thought we'd sneak off. You're okay with that, aren't you?" I asked, worried because it would mean leaving her and Charlie in charge last minute.

"Of course, you silly mare. Now go and pack and I'll rustle up some food for you." She waved me off.

The one thing I loved about Maggie was that she could *rustle* up a meal for ten without blinking. No matter what amount of notice we gave, she had provisions. We had three freezers full of pies, sausage rolls, cakes, all sorts. That was in addition to the two meat freezers. We had long since started to stock our own produce in the campsite shop and it seemed to go down a treat. I recalled a couple of emails asking if we could ship pies. It was something to add to the list of things to do.

I ran up the stairs and into our bedroom. I grabbed a holdall and threw in some summer clothes, then some autumn clothes. I added a couple of waterproofs, just in case. Summer in Scotland didn't necessarily mean we wouldn't encounter every season in the same day.

I added toiletries and dragged the overflowing bag back downstairs.

"Made up a picnic and some items for the fridge," Maggie said, and I saw an overflowing basket by the back door. "You just need to add some wine," she added.

"I'll let Ronan do that."

I sent a quick text to my dad to tell him to contact Charlie when he wanted a lift and explained we were off on our honeymoon. I couldn't just leave without a word, to him at least. By the time I was outside, Max was already in the Land Rover and the caravan door was open. I placed our holdall just inside and went back for the food. Ronan had moved the holdall to the bedroom and he took the basket from me.

"Bloody hell, how long does she think we'll be away?" he asked, and I chuckled.

Maggie was an overfeeder. She was an over-everything really. She loved to look after people as if it were her calling. I'd often remarked she could have been a nun in a previous life. She grabbed me for a hug and then dabbed tears from her eyes.

"Maggie, we are going away for a couple of days at most," Ronan said.

"I know, but it's lovely. You're married and you're off on your honeymoon in Christine," she replied, sniffing.

I wasn't sure what was so tear-jerking about that, but I patted her arm as I passed to raid the cellar of wine.

With bottles clanking under my arms, I climbed into Christine. Ronan was checking gas bottles and *manly* stuff while I secured the booze and food. In one way, it was a shame Christine was so popular among our guests. I'd love to have kept her just for us, but then I wondered if I'd tire of using her. She wasn't up to long journeys, certainly not travelling to France, for example. She was too old for that. I'd had a romantic notion of taking her while Ronan and I travelled through the wine regions with Max. I sighed.

"Are you ready?" Ronan asked.

"Yep. Now where do we go?" I asked.

Ronan scratched his chin, contemplating. "We've been to Skye, so how about we head down to Jura?"

I nodded, never having visited any of the islands except Skye. Jura sounded familiar and I wracked my brain. "Is that where the whisky is made?" I asked.

"Yes, and George Orwell lived there. He wrote *1984* while he was there," Ronan replied.

"Fab, we'll get drunk and read about a country not that dissimilar to what we have now," I said, laughing. I remembered having to read the book back in school. It was a stretch for the imagination, I'd thought at the time. Not so nowadays, of course.

Ronan chuckled. He was a well read man, and that was one thing I loved about him. He'd read a book a week, always something from his library. He'd told me once he'd thought the books to be stuffy and irrelevant, old and smelly. After we'd spent months cleaning and cataloguing them, it seemed to spark his interest again. He had always been a reader as a child but had grown out of it for a while. He had often threatened to pick up one of my erotic romances I shared with Maggie.

I climbed into the Land Rover and with a wave and list of instructions to Maggie, we were off.

I often turned to check Christine was still with us, even though I knew we'd feel it if she had somehow got uncoupled.

"She was a great buy, wasn't she?" I said, smiling and wanting to remind Ronan he thought me mad when I'd first said I wanted to buy her.

"Yes, I concede," he said, chuckling.

I settled back as we crossed Mull heading for the ferry to Oban. We would have two ferry journeys and we were taking a chance, of course, they could be booked up and, because it was summer, we'd have to wait for the next one. I wasn't concerned. There was plenty to do in Oban if we got stuck there for a few hours.

We had been lucky to get booked in on both ferries with only a minimal wait for the second one. When we landed on Jura much later that day, Ronan asked me to search for somewhere that looked suitable to stop. Jura was very barren, more so than Skye, and smaller. There were no official campsites so we were hoping we'd be able to stop at the field opposite the Jura Hotel that's usually set aside for camping in tents. I called ahead and after a little negotiation, they agreed, although we wouldn't have electric hook up. We didn't need that; we had gas to cook and a small battery that would give us lights. After the last trip out where Joe and I got stuck in the snow, Ronan had insisted we added a battery for times when we couldn't get electricity. I was thankful of that. It was, after all, Scotland and the nights, especially on the coast, could still be a little chilly.

Ronan manoeuvred Christine so the bedroom windows faced out to sea, he thought it would be nice in the morning to sit with a cuppa and look out at waves crashing on the rocks. We unhitched the caravan and I put up her awning and set our table and chairs outside. It was warm enough to sit outside and although we knew Max wouldn't run off, we were advised he had to be tethered. He wasn't overly happy but he was on a very long lead that attached to a post screwed into the ground. Before we did anything more, I put the kettle on to boil and we then sat with a cup of tea, admiring the view.

"It's amazing here. Look at the colour of the sea," I said, shaking my head in wonderment. It was the same shade as any I'd seen in a holiday brochure for more far flung places. A beautiful azure blue changing to a vibrant green as it shallowed and most certainly not the brown we'd see back in the south of England.

Between the sea and us was a beach of soft golden sand and I was desperate to sink my bare feet into it. I undid the laces of my Converse and rolled up the legs of my jeans.

"Let's go and paddle," I said, rising from my seat.

Ronan and I took Max down to the nearly deserted beach. Just one other family had camped out at one end and I wondered why it wasn't heaving. It was a beautiful day; the sun was high and strong. It was certainly a sunglasses type of day. Max ran off the lead and straight to the water's edge. He loved to swim in the loch at home but we'd never taken him to a beach before. I made a mental note to check out the times dogs were allowed at some of the local beaches back in Kent. He splashed and bit the waves as they gently broke against the shore.

"How warm do you reckon this is?" I asked, as Ronan and I walked towards it.

"Bloody cold," he replied, and he wasn't wrong.

I let the waves roll over my feet and sucked in a breath sharply as the cold stung my skin. "Jesus," I hissed, running back as quick as I could. "I'm glad I didn't bring my cossie."

It was nice to stroll along the beach, letting the sand slip between my toes. It wasn't as warm on Jura as Mull, which was still many degrees cooler than Kent but I'd grown used to it. I wore just a T-shirt and my jeans, the bottoms of which were wet.

I held onto Ronan's hand as we walked. "I can't believe how beautiful this is. I didn't think to bring my camera, either," I said, cursing myself for forgetting.

Instead, I made Ronan join me in loads of selfies that I sent to Joe and Pam and Del. When I looked back on a couple with the sea in the background, we could have been at any exotic destination in the world.

We didn't leave the campsite. We spent a couple of hours hiking, sitting on the beach just talking, and making love. It was an idyllic couple of days and I was sad to leave. It just wasn't long enough. We returned home with the majority of food still in the basket but happy.

"I promise you, as soon as we have someone who can manage this, you and I are off to the Maldives, or somewhere else where we can do nothing but lie on a beach for two weeks," Ronan said, kissing my temple as I stripped Christine of 'our' things and returned the campsite items.

"I'll hold you to that," I replied. I hadn't had a long holiday in forever. The cruises Harry and I had taken weren't as relaxing as I would have liked. We were off each day on tours and being shuffled from one place to the next, always watching the clock in case we missed the boat. Two weeks in the Maldives sounded like absolute bliss. It was, as Ronan had said, conditional, of course. We couldn't walk away for that length of time.

The film crew had erected all their tracks and whatnots at the front of the property and, that evening, Charlie had us laughing when he told us the crew had an apprentice whose sole job was to check the peafowl's nest every couple of hours to recover missing items. It seemed Clyde had been in his element strutting around, fanning his tail feathers all the while stealing whatever he could.

"He's a clever wee one that bird is" Maggie said. "He puts up his tail as a distraction. It's like that man Patrick Stellars."

"Who?" Ronan asked.

"You know the good-looking man who played the thief. I loved his movies." Maggie had folded her hands together and placed them on the top of her belly. She sighed nostalgically as she thought of Patrick Stellars. Her eyes took on a wistful look while the rest of us just stared at her.

"Peter," I said, shouting as the name came to me. "Peter Sellers, and you mean The Pink Panther."

Ahs sounded around the table as Ronan and Charlie understood. Maggie was still in *Patrick Stellars* mode.

"We should rename Gerald *Kato*," I said, and then laughed, remembering the man that jumped out of wardrobes.

"Anyway, he's been a busy beastie, right enough. He's gallus that yin," Charlie said, bringing us back to Clyde, the pinching peacock.

Charlie, in his wisdom, had written a list, describing items he wasn't sure of the name for. The film crew, who, we were told, were not in the least annoyed, had claimed the majority. In fact, it was a source of entertainment for them. I knew, however, if it continued, Ronan would be having second thoughts about the peafowl.

"I'll get on and make those platforms tomorrow. You see what shiny things we have around that they can gather. It might stop them looking elsewhere," Ronan said. I breathed a sigh of relief that it was an instruction to not send the birds packing.

———

Finding shiny things wasn't as easy as I imagined it to be. We didn't have any CDs or DVDs since we streamed most things. I had found some old costume jewellery in one of the attic rooms. At least, I hoped they were costume. Ronan had just shrugged his shoulders, not recognising the items when I'd shown him. I kept them to one side. Maggie added some old cutlery to the pile. We thought we could drill holes in spoons and hang them from trees.

Ronan came into the kitchen to collect the shiny things. "Didn't you say peacocks get aggressive if they see their reflection?" He held up a serving spoon, looking at his own image.

"Well, yes. That's what they told me. Maybe we won't put that out. He's stealing small things," I said, referring to the fact Clyde seemed to have a liking for anything he could carry rather than anything he could see himself in.

Ronan placed the large spoon to one side. In the box of items he rifled through he found some silver coloured necklaces, brooches, and Maggie had cut some rings from tin foil containers that we thought might be useful as they resembled bracelets, and a handful of old Christmas baubles.

"This should do it," Ronan said, picking up the box. I followed with string and scissors intending to help.

We *decorated* the woods around the site where the birds had nested and were sure to place some items, as well as food, on the wooden platforms Ronan had erected between branches. Peafowl can fly and although their only predator was the fox, we wanted them to be as safe as possible up off the ground. Each day we'd only leave food on the platforms as an enticement.

"I wonder if they'll breed?" I mused, as I continued to hang baubles from branches.

"Just what we need. It'll be like *Peaky Blinders* out here," Ronan replied, laughing at his own joke. "We'll have to be careful they don't start a war with the rest of the misfits."

"Oh, don't call them that. Look at the joy, and money, they bring in," I said, nodding my head and winking at him. I'd scanned the latest reviews and the majority mentioned Colleen or Gerald, not so much Piggy, and I'd started to feel sorry for him.

"I think Piggy might need a friend," I said.

"Nope."

"But—" I started.

"Nope. He's fine, solitary. Doesn't need friends, he's a loner. All pigs are," Ronan lied. I knew it to be a lie because he couldn't quite contain the grin and the skin around his eyes crinkled.

"Don't tell porkies," I said, laughing. "Anyway, I just feel sorry for him."

"Feel sorry all you like. For now, Lizzie—and I really do mean it—no more." Ronan turned back to his hammering and I continued to hang pretty things from branches.

"This reminds me. Carly wants to do a Winter Wonderland. What do you think about Rein—?"

"No!" Ronan said, not even looking at me.

"Let me finish. What do you think about reindeer just for the duration of the event? I'm not talking about keeping them."

I wasn't thinking of keeping them, I didn't think it prudent to have reindeer *and* wild deer in the same environment. Not that I had any knowledge of the carnal desires of either species, but I was sure Ronan wouldn't want them mating.

He didn't answer but that didn't necessarily mean a flat out *no*. We had some bookings over the Christmas period, not for Christmas Day or Boxing Day as we were closed then, but the lead up to and over the New Year. That was all weather dependent, of course. If the snow was bad, there was no telling if anyone would get in towing a caravan. We had tried to limit the bookings to the log cabins only but they had filled up quickly. I think it was the prospect of a basket of sweet goodies on arrival that had been the temptation.

"I think we need to develop the shop a little more. And offer online sales. Add some venison to the produce list as well," I said, randomly.

"I was thinking that. I'll have a chat with the butcher about packaging and things. Maybe you could come up with our brand and logo?" Ronan hammered in the last of the nails and three wooden platforms were ready for occupation.

We gathered up the mess and walked back to the courtyard. It was bustling with agricultural students going about their business, Maggie feeding everyone from a makeshift table that comprised of planks of wood resting on stacked wooden crates, and Charlie talking to a man about a dog.

The students often gathered in the courtyard for their lunch break and it was nice to see them. Ronan had already selected a few he wanted to employ full time when their course was over and we already had a couple who had dropped out, education not being for them, to work with us. They learned more hands-on, so they told us, than sitting at a desk.

"Who is on the salmon run?" I asked, as Ronan put away his tools. It was that time of year for fishing for the estates near famous fish.

"Dan and Eddie. Charlie and I will head down there as well," Ronan said. At the sound of his name, Charlie looked over having finished his conversation about a dog. He shook the man's hand and while his guest left, he walked over to us.

"Any good?" Ronan asked.

"Aye, he'll take the bitch and one of the boys," he replied. I guessed Charlie had been selling some of Bess's puppies even before they'd arrived. She was a top sheepdog and her babies commanded a lot of money, farmers liked to get in early. "Now, what did I hear about fishing?" He beamed having spoken about his favourite sport.

"You make sure to bring one back for ya tea," Maggie called out. "Lizzie can help me gut it." She cackled as she spoke, reminding me, and everyone in the courtyard, including the students, of the time I'd thrown up while trying to gut my first fish.

"Yeah, yeah. I'll leave you to that. There's only so much a city girl is willing to do." I gave her a wink as I teased.

I headed for the office and Ronan went off with Charlie and the boys. I loved that one hour of banter when everyone got together for lunch. It was nice to catch up with the students, even if they moaned about putting on weight, all the while stuffing as many sausage rolls in their mouths as they could.

I settled down at my desk and, at first, just mused on life. It hadn't been that long ago I'd first cleared this office, repainted it so that it was a workable environment. I'd encountered Manuel/Derek and I chuckled at the memory of the fake Spaniard. The last we'd heard, the police were still looking for him in conjunction with a large cannabis farm he'd set up. He'd been arrested, let out on bail, and then had done a runner.

We'd come a long way from those days. I smiled as I opened my computer, ready to input the last week's sales data into my spreadsheet. I'd become a proper little business owner and a fleeting thought crossed my mind. Harry had thought I was nothing more than a glorified housewife, albeit, a super efficient one. *He'd have kittens if he could see me now*. Not that I had any intention of bumping into him, of course.

9

For the first time in its history, the estate was making a profit. I'd shown Ronan my spreadsheet and his response was to open a bottle of champagne and celebrate. Over dinner, we toasted ourselves and all the hard work we'd put in over the previous year.

"You know, it's all down to you," he said, taking my hand and kissing my knuckles.

"No, it's down to all of us," I replied, smiling at my family sitting around the table.

"He's right, lass. We didnae ken what to do until you came along," Charlie said, and I was a little surprised he dabbed the corner of his eye with his rotten hankie.

"You're not crying are you, ya bampot?" Maggie said, swatting at his arm and Charlie laughed.

"I mean it, Mags. This old hoose woulda fallen doon around our ears," he replied.

"Wow, well, thank you. And long may it continue," I said, raising my glass. I still thought it a joint effort even if some of us were dragged along; I glanced at Ronan and smiled.

We were eating poached salmon with the most beautiful homemade dill sauce, new potatoes, carrots and peas. I'd spoken to Maggie about batch making her sauces, we were going to bottle them and sell them in the campsite shop. In addition, we'd all agreed we would offer an online shop as well. I'd been researching, we could buy small insulated cases to box the items up and courier them out.

The food shop would be another string to our bow; our growing empire as Maggie called it.

"Maggie's Marmalade, don't forget," she said. She made the most divine marmalade and jams and she insisted, rightly so, that her name was on the jar.

"Maggie's Magnificent Jams, as well," I added, coming up with names for the produce.

We laughed as our suggestions got more ridiculous, especially when Charlie wanted to add something to his name. Charlie's Cakes just wasn't cutting it for Maggie and me.

"If you want tae bleeding make them, you can call them what you like," she admonished, folding her arms over her bosom for emphasis.

After we'd cleared the dishes, Ronan and I took our wine to sit on the terrace. Clyde was sitting on the stone balustrade, looking all regal and as if he really did belong. It wasn't long before Colleen, Gerald, and Piggy joined us. Piggy flopped to the floor waiting for his tummy rub and Gerald butted the wall.

"I think he has a screw loose," I said.

"If he didn't before, he does now. I wonder what he thinks he'll achieve by headbutting a stone wall?"

"We might have to upgrade the pool noodles," I added. Gerald, who was meant to have been a miniature goat, was growing up fast. When Clyde squawked, Gerald fainted. We laughed; even Colleen seemed to smile along with us.

"How did this happen, huh?" Ronan asked quietly, while settling back on a seat and resting his feet on the small table.

"How did what happen?" I asked.

"All this." He waved his arm around.

"Well, your mum was born to someone quite wealthy. Then she did the dirty with a nasty and you came along.

Then you met me in a bar, forgot about me, then remembered me, and the rest…? I guess the rest is history," I said, laughing.

Ronan placed his arm around my shoulders. "So what's next?" he asked.

"Other than the shop? I think we just carry on as we are for a while. I'm sure something will present itself in a few months. Or the chimney stacks will fall down," I said. We both looked up, just in case.

I snuggled into his side, content with my lot. I had a wonderful husband. I had Maggie and Charlie, who were more than parents to us both, and we had a menagerie of oddballs as friends, pets, and relatives.

Life is just grand, I thought.

The End

Keep reading to learn a little more about that Mountford Diamond Ronan speaks about!

THE FREEDOM DIAMOND

The Freedom Diamond - Chapter One

My name is Dorothy Mountford, the year was nineteen hundred and twelve and I was about to embark on the great ship, *Titanic*. I was exceptionally fortunate that, at only twenty years old, I travelled alone and in first class. I thought I might pretend to be a married woman, of course. It really wasn't the done thing for a woman to travel so far without a chaperone. I refused my father's offer, or perhaps it was his version of insistence, of taking staff with me, and with good reason. I despised my father, he just didn't realise that.

My family spent months trying to dissuade me from this adventure. Thankfully, they were unsuccessful. I shall continue my travels, writing my journals, and experiencing a life many could only dream about.

This journey, however, was a particularly special one.

"You have them both, don't you?" Ernest asked.

I sighed and patted his cheek. "My darling, you need to stop worrying so much. I have them both, secured in my luggage."

Ernest was anxious that I'd take great care of the two ceramic figurines. I thought them quite hideous to be honest, but he'd made them, and I would, indeed, take great care of them.

"And you know what to do when you arrive?" he asked.

I was tempted to sigh, yet again, and perhaps pat the other cheek.

"Ernest, I'm not sure how many times we have been over this plan. I know what to do when I arrive. You've no need to continue to worry, it's all perfectly mapped out, up here," I said, pointing to my head.

I shivered as the evening drew in. The air was damp from an earlier storm and Southampton wasn't perhaps the most pleasant of places for our meet. However,

Ernest had insisted on the secrecy, even though we were far from prying eyes.

"Shall we take a walk? It's becoming chilly," I asked.

Arm in arm, we walked back to where I was to stay for the evening. Ernest seemed particularly on edge, more so than normal.

"You've sorted your passage?" I asked.

"Yes, within a week or so, I'll join you."

"And you have enough funds, Ernest?" I asked, knowing he wasn't comfortable with talking about money.

"I do, now, how has your day been?" he answered, changing the subject completely.

We chatted as he walked me to a wonderful little boarding house I'd found. I could stay in a hotel, but I liked the anonymity it offered. I'd used a false name, of course. There was no reason for anyone to know who I was; my family name often preceded me.

Lord Mountford wasn't a particularly well-liked individual in the business world, nor the political one he so often frequented. Many times I would disassociate myself from my father, and I suspected a complete disownment would follow at some point. For Ernest's and my plan to work, I needed to keep my father on my side for a little longer, even if it galled me to do so.

I hugged Ernest, despite the stiffness in his body. He may have fallen, or been forced, from grace but he was still full of manners. Hugging a lady in a street wasn't appropriate in his mind. I didn't care; perhaps that was my downfall. I hitched the folds of my skirt, noticing how dirty the hem had become and walked the steps to the front door. I gave Ernest a slight wave as he slipped away.

The next day, I was to embark on a magnificent journey, a dangerous journey. I climbed into bed with a stomach bubbling full of excitement.

The following morning I was collected from my boarding house, my luggage was transported to the dock, and I stood and looked in awe at the structure before me. The *Titanic* was most certainly an impressive vessel. The dockside was bustling, porters and passengers were busy with loading luggage or saying goodbye to loved ones. Before I took the first steps onto the gangplank, I looked across the concrete dock and saw Ernest in the distance. He gently raised his hand in a wave before bringing his fingertips to his lips. I smiled, although not sure he'd fully see.

"Ma'am, may I escort you to your cabin?" I was asked.

I turned to see a porter standing midway along the entrance. I handed him my paperwork and he gave me a short bow of his head. I followed him. I bade a good morning to fellow passengers as we walked, eventually arriving at my cabin. The walls were lined with mahogany; a plush carpet decorated with golden swirls gave the room a very opulent feel. I walked over to the bed and ran my hand over the brocade bedspread.

"Will your maid be joining you?" I was asked, as my luggage was pushed into the room.

"No, I shall be travelling alone."

"Perhaps you would like some help to unpack?"

"I'll be fine, thank you for your help."

I wanted him to leave so I could familiarise myself with the room and store my things away.

He bowed at the waist and backed out the room. I couldn't fault the politeness of the stewards at all, although I didn't like the deference. That was something my father courted, not me.

I opened my luggage and stored away my clothes; perhaps I should have brought a maid as I noticed some creases to my favourite dress. Still, I was more than capable of taking care of myself, and I was sure there would be a laundry on board.

Lastly, I unwrapped the two figurines Ernest had given me. I held them both in my hands and stared at them. My future lay there. A slow smile formed as I thought of the small, ceramic naked women. They were particularly risqué and that had been Ernest's fault. I guessed he had thought they'd not draw attention being so inappropriate, but I loved them. I loved the way he had captured the curves and the detail of a woman's body. I should have thought to ask him how he had acquired such knowledge. I hadn't been aware of any relationship, but then he had spent most of his life in India.

I placed both in the small safe that was conveniently located in a closet, but then changed my mind. I took one out and placed it on a small table, surrounded by two chairs, in the middle of the room. It would be fun to see the look of shock, I imagined I would encounter, when my room was cleaned.

A small welcome document had been left in my cabin and I sat and read. Available for my leisure was a swimming bath, I wasn't sure I would spend any time there, a gymnasium, a Parisian café, which looked very tempting, among other things. A cup of tea would be most certainly welcomed.

I found the ship easy to navigate and spent a little time exploring. I leaned over the railing and looked at the still busy dockside before making my way to the café for mid-morning tea. No matter how much I wanted to shed the life I'd been brought up in, mid-morning, and afternoon, tea would always be a must. Sitting with my mother in the sunroom at home, or on the terrace on a bright summer's morning was the highlight of my day.

"Lady Mountford, I thought that was you," I heard, and I winced.

I turned to see an elderly gentleman with his wife by his side.

"Lord Attenthrall, Lady Attenthrall, how wonderful to see you."

I greeted the couple and accepted their brief air kiss to my cheek.

"Your father mentioned you were taking this trip, we promised we'd look out for you because he worried you were travelling alone. I have a maid who can help with your needs," Lady Attenthrall said.

"That's very kind of you. I'm sure I will be fine; I'm quite excited by this adventure. But I will be sure to call upon you if I need help," I replied. That seemed to satisfy her, and she smiled.

We walked to the café together and it hurt my heart to see how disrespectful Lord Attenthrall was towards the staff. His demanding and bullish manner assured we were seated at the best table, but I didn't like the man, or his overbearing and social climbing wife. Mother had often told me she'd been a mistress to a married man before ensnaring the Lord. And she was at least twenty years his junior. They'd caused quite a scandal, if I remember, and I'd laughed at the outrage.

I sipped on my tea and tuned out of Lady Attenthrall's gossip. I dearly wanted to tell her how she'd been the source of many an afternoon tea chat, but I smiled, nodded, and gently laughed, when required to do so. Had I known the Attenthralls would be on board, I would have taken measures to avoid them.

The Freedom Diamond is a short novelette originally written as part of an anthology to celebrate an author signing in Belfast, the home of the Titanic.
You can read the rest here
mybook.to/TheFreedomDiamond

GET A FREE NOVELLA

If you'd like to read, Evelyn, a novella that accompanies the Fallen Angel series but can be as a standalone, simply sign up for my newsletter and you'll receive notification on how to download.
https://www.subscribepage.com/v8h1g0

ABOUT THE AUTHOR

Tracie Podger currently lives in Kent, UK with her husband and a rather obnoxious cat called George. She's a Padi Scuba Diving Instructor with a passion for writing. Tracie has been fortunate to have dived some of the wonderful oceans of the world where she can indulge in another hobby, underwater photography. She likes getting up close and personal with sharks.

Tracie likes to write in different genres. Her Fallen Angel series and its accompanying books are mafia romance and full of suspense. A Virtual Affair, Letters to Lincoln and Jackson are angsty, contemporary romance, and Gabriel, A Deadly Sin and Harlot are thriller/suspense. The Facilitator books are erotic romance. Just for a change, Tracie also decided to write a couple of romcoms and a paranormal suspense! All can be found at: author.to/TraciePodger

ALSO BY TRACIE PODGER

Fallen Angel, Part 1

Fallen Angel, Part 2

Fallen Angel, Part 3

Fallen Angel, Part 4

Fallen Angel, Part 5

Fallen Angel, Part 6

The Fallen Angel Box Set

Evelyn - A novella to accompany the Fallen Angel Series

Rocco – A novella to accompany the Fallen Angel Series

Robert – To accompany the Fallen Angel Series

Travis – To accompany the Fallen Angel Series

Taylor & Mack – To accompany the Fallen Angel Series

Angelica – To accompany the Fallen Angel Series

A Virtual Affair – A standalone

Gabriel – A standalone

The Facilitator – A duet

The Facilitator, part 2 – A duet

A Deadly Sin – A standalone

Harlot – A standalone

Letters to Lincoln – A standalone

Jackson – A standalone

The Freedom Diamond – A novella

Limp Dicks & Saggy Tits

Cold Nips & Frosty Bits

Posh Frocks & Peacocks

STALKER LINKS

https://www.facebook.com/TraciePodgerAuthor/
http://www.TraciePodger.com
https://www.instagram.com/traciepodger/

Printed in Great Britain
by Amazon